She was a sure target for rape until Nick Carter stepped in . . .

The girl screamed again as the tall man tossed her aside. An outraged man with stern, Teutonic features, he muttered something unintelligible and rushed at me, his hands aimed at my neck.

I dropped into a crouch and laid a sharp right into his gut, which barely fazed him. But a hand slice to the side of his neck staggered him, and the right he aimed at my head missed by a foot.

Stunned, he groped for an inside pocket and found a small, blue automatic. I brought my left foot up and around in a fast roundhouse kick which sent the cheap pistol clattering down the pavement. For an instant, the man and I exchanged stares. I sensed he wasn't one to take defeat well, but he would take it.

"Don't push your luck," I said.

He didn't respond, but turned and ran down the block, holding his stomach in a vain attempt to stop the pain. The girl was sitting on the sidewalk, her legs curled under her, her eyes as big as silver dollars. I extended a hand to her, and she took it.

NICK CARTER IS IT!

Dedicated to the men of the
Secret Services of the
United States of America

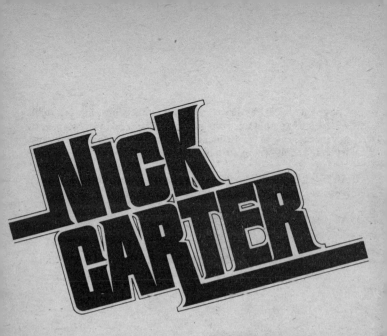

NICK CARTER

CAULDRON OF HELL

CHARTER
NEW YORK

A Division of Charter Communications Inc.
A GROSSET & DUNLAP COMPANY
51 Madison Avenue
New York, New York 10010

An Ace Charter Original.

First Ace Charter Printing November 1981
Published simultaneously in Canada
Manufactured in the United States of America

2 4 6 8 0 9 7 5 3 1

CAULDRON OF HELL

ONE

Although June was but halfway gone, the thick heat of summer had already spread over New York. Winos and derelicts who in winter huddled in doorways and alleys lounged on midtown curbs and the hoods of cars, drinking and laughing with one another over jokes only they understood. A ten-dollar whore, too raunchy for the massage parlors and in any case unwilling to pay half her wages to the landlord, fanned herself with a bit of tarpaper torn from a bundle at the foot of the building under construction on Seventh Avenue. She smiled as I walked by, tucked in her tummy and asked, "Wanna go out?"

"I've *been* out."

I had, too, and very good it was. After two weeks in the Outer Hebrides of Scotland finding out why so many fatal "accidents" were plaguing the new herring fleet, I was primed for a few days off. In three nights in New York, I had seen as many shows and had twice as many good meals. The one I had just finished was exquisite. Orsini's *timbale rigatoni* and fish galantine were as marvelous as I remembered, and the half bottle of Val d'Anapo, better. I was in no mood for a ten-dollar whore, especially on a hot summer's night on Seventh Avenue.

"Come on, man, it's too hot to argue. Ten bucks."

"Some other time."

"Let's go to your hotel," she insisted, following me down the block, while street lamps cast jagged shadows across the ground floor of the skeletonlike building-to-be.

"How'd you know I'm staying in a hotel? And what do I get for my money?"

"I knew it! A cop!" She whirled and stalked back to the bundle of tarpaper, sitting on it and fanning herself all the harder for the effort of having chased me a few paces. I smiled. Even while being a pain in the ass, New Yorkers are colorful.

Eighth Avenue was choked with traffic, all northbound out of the theater district and jammed by the forever-packed Columbus Circle. I walked in the opposite direction from my hotel, in search of an hour's slumming. Three days of Broadway theater and gourmet food and the prospect of a new assignment in the morning filled me with the urgent longing for an Irish bar. There was a Blarney Stone on Eighth and Fifty-fourth, and a Phillies game on cable TV. A shot of Chivas, a short beer and a half hour of Pete Rose seemed the best way to top off my brief vacation.

I saw her as she walked south on the west side of the avenue, her flame-red hair and easy grace seeming out of place in the seedy neighborhood. She was a tall woman who hardly appeared twenty-five, and she looked around her, tossing her hair wildly but failing to notice the two men who followed her onto Fifty-fifth Street. That block was dark, dominated by high-rise apartment construction, and lifeless. I couldn't guess why she was going down it, but could think of any number of reasons why she might be pursued. The Blarney Stone would have to wait.

I crossed the avenue against the light, picking my way through the stream of yellow cabs. The girl walked briskly, unaware of the danger. Her well-muscled thighs rippled beneath the thin fabric of her red dress. I was not a native New Yorker, but knew the city well enough to realize that a girl with her looks shouldn't walk down a deserted street alone. The men following her speeded up, the taller of the pair taking a last drag on a slender brown cigarette and tossing it aside.

When I entered the block she was in the middle of it, halfway to Ninth Avenue. A stubby office building, some of its windows blown out, was in the early stages of demolition. Two large industrial dumpsters filled with plaster, rotten wood and scrap steel stood in the street, forming with the building a shadowy corridor through which pedestrians were forced. The girl stepped into it, and her pursuers broke into a run.

I went into the street and ran outside the row of parked cars and trucks. I heard a scream, a loud one, and then two smaller noises, rather like a lamb acknowledging the inevitability of slaughter. I rounded the dumpsters and saw them. Both had pasty, pallid skin. One was twice the size of the other, and both seemed in pretty good shape. The tall one wore ill-fitting jeans and cowboy boots, and the other a loose-fitting double-knit suit. One had his arms around the girl's waist while the other struggled to pull a ring from her finger. I stepped in.

"Is this a private mugging, or can anyone take part?" I asked.

The short man was the one tugging at the ring. Startled, he whirled at me, an adept left hand missing my cheek by inches.

I sidestepped the punch and countered with a left of my own. I got him just below the eye, spinning him around and setting him up for a crashing right which caved in his mouth, teeth snapping away from bone, dropping him to the pavement, unconscious.

The girl screamed again as the tall man tossed her aside. An outraged man with stern, Teutonic features, he muttered something unintelligible and rushed at me, his hands aimed at my neck.

I dropped into a crouch and laid a sharp right into his gut, which barely fazed him. But a hand slice to the side of his neck staggered him, and the right he aimed at my head missed by a foot.

Stunned, he groped for an inside pocket and found a small, blue automatic. I brought my left foot up and around in a fast roundhouse kick which sent the cheap pistol clattering down the pavement. For an instant, the man and I exchanged stares. I sensed he wasn't one to take defeat well, but he would take it.

"Don't push your luck," I said.

He didn't respond, but turned and ran down the block, holding his stomach in a vain attempt to stop the pain. The girl was sitting on the sidewalk, her legs curled under her, her eyes as big as silver dollars. I extended a hand to her, and she took it.

"Are you okay?"

"Yeah . . . I think so."

I helped her up. She was taller than I realized, and in reasonably good condition for the ordeal she had just been through. I brushed a patch of plaster dust from her hip.

"Do you always walk down streets like this in the middle of the night?" She took up where I left off and, finding the dust far too ingrained to remove with a few swipes of the hand, scowled at her sleek dress.

"I saw them following you. Getting involved was my civic duty. Can we go someplace else? I'm tired of watching this guy bleed."

He *was* bleeding, too; a real mess lying on the pavement, not even quivering.

"I was on my way home," she said. "I just got an apartment on Fifty-third and Ninth. I haven't gotten too attuned to the neighborhood yet, and don't know which streets aren't safe."

"May I walk you home?"

"Yes," she said. "Let's get out of here."

She took my arm and held it tightly as we walked to her building. That area, called Clinton by the local politicos, was the up-and-coming section of Manhattan. Most other residential neighborhoods had grown too expensive for the average man or woman.

"I've got to thank you," she said.

"Civic duty, like I told you."

"You're very good in a fight. Are you a cop or something?"

I shook my head. "Archaeologist," I said. "My name is Paul Rainsford."

"Rita Brennan. Do archaeologists always know how to fight?"

"Did you ever spend ten months alone in the wilds of Uganda?"

"Not really."

"You learn how to fight. Actually, martial arts is my form of exercise. Everyone else in my line of work, if he stays in shape at all, jogs or plays squash. Squash is a terrific game, but it doesn't do you a lot of good when two punks are trying to change your shirt size."

"I see," she responded, nodding her head.

"What do *you* do? I would guess emergency room doctor. You didn't exactly cave in when I rearranged that guy's face."

She smiled when I said "doctor" instead of "nurse." "I'm a newspaperwoman," she went on. "I work for United American News Service, so I guess I've seen my share of blood and gore."

"Reporter?"

"Photographer. I was in the UANS London Bureau for two years, and now I'm going to be based in New York. I'll fly wherever they need me. My building is right over here."

She led me into a brand-new, dark stone and tinted-glass

box perhaps thirty-five stories tall. The housing crush in New York being what it was, apartments were being occupied even as piles of ceiling tile stood about the lobby awaiting installation. A concierge sat in a low-stone enclosure watching the ball game I had so narrowly missed.

Rita's apartment was on the west side of the fifteenth floor, a smart, two-bedroom flat with a view of the Hudson River and New Jersey. The windows were large, and the panorama beyond them spectacular. There wasn't much in the way of furniture—just a wicker couch with two matching chairs, and a white Formica Parson's table.

She sighed in relief as the bolt was turned behind us. "Thank God I'm home. I know it doesn't look like much, but right now it feels like a palace."

"Do you always take home men you meet on the streets?" I asked.

"Only if they've just saved my life."

"Which happens all the time, I suppose."

"Twice a week at least. You'll stay a while, I hope. Why don't you make us some drinks. I take vodka on the rocks. There's a bottle of Stolichnaya in the refrigerator. Find something for youself. I want to change my clothes."

I watched her as she walked to the bedroom, her fingers already reaching for the zipper at the back of her dress. Rita seemed to be taking the events of the evening in stride. There is, in New York, a certain sense of the inevitability of trouble. And she was, as well, a newspaperwoman who presumably was accustomed to being in tight spots. I made the drinks and took a seat on the couch to wait for her.

A pink folding telephone sat on the table with an extra-long cord snaking across the room to a baseboard plug. I dialed a number in New York.

I said, "This is Killmaster N3. I put a guy down on Fifty-fifth between Eighth and Ninth. Find out who the hell he is, would you? I'm at 703 West Fifty-third, apartment 15G." I gave my contact Rita's telephone number, then added with a smile, "It looks like I'll be staying the night."

TWO

Rita savored her vodka like a man, rolling it around in her mouth before swallowing. She wore cutoff jeans and an oversized tee shirt emblazoned with the logo of the Broadway show "A Chorus Line." Curled up on the other side of the couch from me, she looked even more beautiful than before.

"If I didn't make it clear before, let me say it again—thanks. You saved my life."

I shrugged off the notion. "It was most likely a run-of-the-mill purse snatching."

"Okay, so you saved my purse. In any event, I'm grateful."

"Forget it. Tell me about yourself."

"No. You first."

"What's to say? I'm an associate of the New York Museum of Prehistory—"

"Do you live in the city?"

"No. I live in D.C., an apartment in Georgetown. But I'm on the road nearly all the time, and seldom get to stay there."

"What are you doing in New York?"

"Just resting. I'm on my way home from a couple of

months in Scotland. We have a dig going there . . . a paleolithic hunting village in the Outer Hebrides that was discovered last year. I was pretty exhausted, so I checked into the Plaza for a couple of days to wind down."

"And ran into me, right? Some relief."

"I have no complaints so far."

I sipped my Chivas Regal and took a moment to appraise her. There was little chance I would have complaints. In the soft light of her apartment, her dark red hair and large brown eyes were enthralling; her slim, soft lips an invitation. Rita had large breasts which gently rose with every breath, and fine, long legs. She didn't resemble any newspaperwomen I had ever seen, with the possible exception of Brenda Starr. The thought made me laugh.

"What's so funny?" she asked.

"Just the thought that my running into you was in any way an inconvenience," I said, telling no lie whatsoever.

"Then I'm not keeping you from someone," she said quietly.

"I have no one to be kept from. I was going to watch a ball game, but the hell with it."

"There's a TV in the bedroom."

I shook my head. If I was going into her bedroom, the last thing I wanted to see was Pete Rose. And I was fully prepared to go into Rita's bedroom. There had been a long dry spell while I was in Scotland. The Outer Hebrides are many things, but not a spot to meet women. And being a Killmaster for the super-secret American intelligence agency AXE *does* give you some other obligations. On my last mission, there was neither available women nor the time to enjoy them. Rita was a gift from the gods and very welcome. Beating up on two thugs to get her was no bother at all.

She finished her drink and, in the course of getting another, sat closer to me on the couch.

"You were going to tell me about yourself." I said.

"A pretty ordinary life in my business. I've been working

for UANS three years now, ever since I got out of college."

"Where'd you go?"

"Sarah Lawrence. You?"

"Columbia, all the way."

"So you have a doctorate? Dr. Paul Rainsford, is it? That's pretty impressive."

"It got me a job. I work as an adjunct in the Smithsonian, too."

"Which explains the Georgetown apartment."

"What have you covered?" I asked.

"Most of the time, nothing of interest. But I happened to be in Sofia when the Iran-Iraq War broke out, and hopped down to Baghdad to cover it. I spent a month-and-a-half on the front. I'm sure you've seen some of my photos in the papers."

"Probably. I read a lot."

"I'll show them to you anyway. I'm kind of proud of what I've done."

She ran into the second bedroom and emerged in a few seconds with a large, leather portfolio. With Rita sitting close enough for our legs to touch, she showed me photographs of Russian-made Goryunov 7.62mm heavy machine guns, their Iraqi gunners showing them off as an American fisherman might display a trout. Rita had pictures of proud young Arabs patting the stiletto noses of Mikoyan Mig-23 fighters, and of civilians running from the blazing fires of the Abadan refinery.

"You're very good," I said when she was done. "I've seen a few of them in the paper . . . that one with the jet plane, for example."

"The Mig."

"If you say so. My specialty is digging, not war. I like the faces in your photographs. You're very good at capturing expressions."

Beaming with pride, she put aside the leather case and twisted toward me.

"I'm good at a lot more than that," she said.

Rita pulled me to her, crushing her breasts against my chest, her hands roaming my body. She was electric and totally alive. This was new for a change; she was the agressor. I hugged her as her mouth sought mine, her tongue sweeping inside and dueling with my own.

Rita's hands dropped to my belt. Abruptly, I stood. She was startled, and asked, "What's the matter?"

I said nothing, but slipped one arm behind her and a hand between her legs. Grasping her buttocks and cradling her in my arms, I lifted her and carried her to the bedroom.

Several small, white clouds drifted across the morning sky, and 727s en route into LaGuardia skimmed them, noiseless through the west windows of Rita's apartment. She lay on my arm, a hand resting lightly on my thigh, her hair a halo about her. She had been in that position an hour; my arm was cramping.

"Move," I said gently, freeing my arm and rubbing it.

"Hey," she protested.

"Be quiet. I hurt. You're too much for me."

"It was more like the other way around," she said with a laugh, turning toward me until her left breast rested on my skin.

"You just have a thing for older men."

"I have a thing for you, and you're not that much older than me. Are you sure you're unattached?"

"Positive. I'm always too busy to form attachments."

"Good. You'll make a terrific father for my children."

"Moving a little fast, aren't we?" I laughed, "considering you've only known me for twelve hours."

"Fourteen," she replied, nodding at the clock at the same time as she pushed her way to her feet. "I have to go to the ladies' room. Keep the bed warm for me, will you?"

I looked around the room as she padded off. There wasn't much time for scrutiny the night before. Rita's bedroom was a plain white cubicle with an old standing lamp and a long, low dresser. The closet was built in, and the only other furniture was a double mattress laid out by the window. Cardboxes like those in the living room held long-playing records, mostly classical music and opera, and a digital clock radio sat on the floor next to an extension phone and a small TV.

The phone rang while she was still in the bathroom.

"Get that, would you?" she called.

"Get it yourself. I know better than to answer a lady's telephone during the breakfast hour."

"I don't have any attachments, either. Please get the phone."

"It's a matter of principle. You don't get to be an older man without learning something."

The toilet flushed and Rita padded back in to answer the phone, a look of mild annoyance on her face.

"It's for you, *Dr. Rainsford,*" she said, handing over the receiver.

I listened for a moment, then hung up.

"How'd the museum get my phone number?" she asked.

"I left a message at my hotel last night. I thought I might have a meeting to go to this morning."

"And you do?"

"Yeah, in an hour."

She sighed, and knelt over me. "I was planning to make love to you again, and then make you breakfast."

"So?" I asked, knowing the answer.

"Breakfast will have to wait," she replied, and lowered her head to my loins.

My senses were so attuned to the sound and smell of Rita Brennan, that when I got back to my suite at the Plaza an hour later, I wasn't able to immediately identify Hawk's cigar aroma.

David Hawk was director and chief of operations at AXE.

Once a field operator like myself, with the reputation among department old-timers of having been as tough as nails and twice as ornery, he remained formidable even into his early sixties. I respected him immensely, and maybe feared him a little. His fatherly attitude softened him a bit, and he sincerely seemed to care about the men who worked for him. I was sure of one thing—when Hawk left his Dupont Circle, Washington office, something rather important was in the wind.

I let myself into the suite. He acknowledged my appearance with a wave of the cigar, a large, foul bunch of twisted weed that smoked like a volcano and smelled worse.

"Good morning, Carter. That was nice work you did in Scotland."

"Thank you, sir."

"I guess you did a pretty nice job last night, too," he said, with no expression.

"Not bad, sir."

"Who is she?"

"Rita Brennan. Says she's a photographer for UANS, just transferred here from London."

"That'll be easy enough to check."

Indeed it should. AXE had for years used the cover of the Amalgamated Press and Wire Services and knew everyone in the trade. If she wasn't what she said she was, it would show up right away.

"I rescued her from two muggers, sir. She was grateful."

"Hmm, yes," Hawk replied. "As far as the mugger you left on Fifty-fifth street goes, he was gone by the time we got there, and it was only five minutes after you called."

"Had the cops picked him up?"

"No. He just disappeared. Just a little blood on the pavement."

"I can assure you he didn't get up and walk away on his own."

"They usually don't when you're through with them,"

Hawk said, flicking cigar ash onto the Plaza's carpet. "Do you think this girl is setting you up?"

I thought a moment. "It's possible. If she checks out to be a legitimate UANS photographer, I would assume she's not setting me up. I've seen her pictures in the paper, but that means nothing. I just don't know for sure yet."

"Well, we'll know soon," Hawk said. "Right now I've got a new assignment for you, and it's a beauty."

He didn't smile when he said the last word. And if I knew Hawk, he was probably right. It was going to be a beauty.

THREE

"What's up?" I asked.

"Over here." Hawk led me to the coffee table, across which he had spread a mammoth topographical map and a passel of photographs. It showed mountainous terrain with few habitations, sliced by the arc of the Amur River, the long-disputed border between Chinese Manchuria and the Soviet Union.

He pressed a fingertip against a spot on the River. "That's where it impacted."

"It?"

"A large meteorite flying a deep-space trajectory entered the earth's atmosphere and landed there." He tapped the spot with his finger. "It hit ten miles inside the Russian border and made a pretty good crater. Burned a lot of woodland, too. Here's a photo of the region."

Hawk produced an eight by ten glossy print that bore the unmistakable grid marks of satellite reconnaissance. In the center of a huge patch of forested hills seemingly forgotten by man, sat a circle of burned-out woods a quarter mile in diameter resembling a gigantic bullet hole.

"The impact was picked up by seismographs in New York," Hawk went on, "but only as a gentle tremor. Deep-space meteorites are made of lighter stuff than the ones we get in our solar system, or so I'm told. That may be why the Russians haven't shown interest. They may not know it happened."

"If I may ask, why are *we* interested?"

"I'm coming to that. Anyway, the Agros V mineral discovery satellite got a shot of this thing . . . tracked it right out of the goddamn sky too."

"Tracked it? Why would a mineral discovery satellite track a meteorite?"

"Have you ever heard of lidanium, Nick?"

I thought a moment. "A heavy element, only existed in theory until two years ago, and now exists only in the lab. It's made in that big cyclotron in Belgium, I think, and costs something like a million an ounce."

"A million five," Hawk corrected, "only we've never gotten anything like an ounce. Try half a milligram. This stuff is so rare and so expensive to make that we took to looking for it in space. Lidanium is known to exist in some quantity in the cores of deep-space meteorites. The Agros V satellite was programmed to look for lidanium, among other things. It went absolutely wild when that meteorite flew by. There must be fifty pounds of lidanium in that rock."

I tried to look impressed, even though I hadn't the faintest idea why anyone would be interested in lidanium. I try to keep up with developments in many fields, but molecular physics is not one. I had read an article in the London *Times* about the Belgium cyclotron, and recalled the slim information about lidanium.

"Do you know the value of lidanium?"

"No, sir. I'm sorry."

"You're not expected to be an expert in *everything*, Nick," Hawk laughed. "I didn't know myself until our experts told me."

"What is it?"

"It absorbs radioactivity like a wino sucking up cheap port. We think that one pound of lidanium can absorb all the ambient radiation from a major reactor incident or breach of containment in a nuclear waste dump."

Now I *was* impressed, and showed it. Hawk seemed gratified. He liked it when his operatives showed appreciation for the value of their work.

"This stuff could solve many problems," Hawk continued. "It's perfect shielding for the reactors in nuclear-powered ships, for one thing."

I nodded. "With lidanium, nuclear energy would prove to be the perfectly clean power source we used to hear about."

"Right! And there are, of course, applications in the event of nuclear war. I won't play down the importance of getting the lidanium out of that meteorite. The White House wants it, and that's good enough for me."

"Me, too."

"You will continue as Dr. Paul Rainsford. It worked in Scotland, and it will work in Manchuria. There's a dig going on not far from the impact point on the Chinese side of the border and . . ." He hesitated portentiously, "we're working with the Chinese on this."

I frowned, and Hawk replied "Yes, I agree. ORG is into it again."

He referred to the Overseas Responsibility Group, a factor within the State Department that believed it was necessary for the United States to trust one of the major communist powers. In the 1960s, ORG wanted us to befriend the Russians and play them against the Chinese, if possible. Now it was the other way around. ORG is commonly held to mean "orgasm," implying "jerk off," among AXE operatives. Our scorn means nothing to them. They often have the ear of the White House, and we have to put up with them.

"Do we have to go through this again?" I asked, recalling numerous occasions when the ORG hotshots nearly got our guys killed.

"Yes, we do. The Chinese will go along with our cover

story. They'll provide assistance and backup as far as the Amur River border, and when we get the lidanium, we'll share it with them."

I said nothing. It was hopeless.

"Orders are orders, Nick."

"Of course, sir."

"The dig is in Kumara, a border town and fishing village on the Chinese side of the river. The New York Museum of Prehistory is mounting an expedition to the site. You'll play archaeologist for a few days, then when the time is right, you'll slip across the border with an assistant, get the lidanium, and bring it back to the Chinese side."

"I don't need an assistant," I said.

"I know, but the Chinese insist on it. I guess they want to make sure you come back."

"Where am I supposed to go? You're giving me a choice between Chinese Manchuria and Soviet Siberia. Of course I'm going to come back to the Chinese side. I like their food better than the Russians'."

Hawk smiled, and said, "Your contact at the museum is Andrea Regan. Know her?"

"I've heard of her."

"She'll know who you really are, and she's going along for the same reason the museum is and—"

"We give them a lot of money," I cut in.

He ignored the comment and continued. "I hear she's not easy to get along with."

"That's just great. With the Russians, the Chinese, and her, I should have a terrific time on this mission."

"*Vita brevis*, Nick," Hawk said, blowing a large cloud of vile tobacco smoke in my direction.

FOUR

The New York Museum of Prehistory was housed in the bulky old McKim, Mead & White granite block which had for the first eighty years of the twentieth century stood on the corner of Sixty-seventh Street and Central Park West. Terra cotta lions scowled from the cornices, and six Corinthian columns cast deep shadows the length of the facade, giving the museum even more of a somber tone.

I went inside, flashing my staff card to get past the ticket barrier. The large main hall was filled with groups of people milling about the new exhibit. The massive hall was dominated by fiberglass replicas of the gigantic granite menhirs, ceremonial monuments from the neolithic period found in Carnac in southern Brittany. Picking my way around the enigmatic megaliths and the groups of the curious gawking at them, I left the main hall, traversed a large and a small corridor, and took the staff elevator to the fourth floor and the Department of Vertebrate Paleontology.

Unlike the gleaming marble floors and spotless display cases of the public areas, the staff offices of the museum were

19

barely functional and not at all attractive. I found one to which was taped a file card bearing the simple legend *Regan*. I knocked on a green wood door and went inside.

I recognized the good doctor from having seen her around the building. She was tall, with long honey blonde hair that she usually wore tied back into a pony tail. Bodily, Andrea was what used to be called "a sturdy woman," probably with a lot of Nordic blood. Her shoulders were wide, as were her hips, but she had a flat stomach and immense breasts that she took great pains to conceal. A body like hers would have to be a hindrance in her line of work, where, given that she was a scientist, everything had to be taken seriously. I understood the reasoning behind the reputation for her contrariness.

"Dr. Regan?" I asked.

She had been bending over a large plastic tray that normally holds cat litter. She turned with a smile which quickly changed to a frown.

"I've seen you before," she said suspiciously.

"Carter. Nick Carter. I'm told you're expecting me."

Andrea straightened up and shook my hand, making no pretense about her reluctance to work with me. I was accustomed to this treatment. In Scotland, my "colleagues" deeply resented having "Dr. Paul Rainsford" in their midst, but as long as AXE bankrolled their expedition, they had no legitimate cause to complain.

"Call me Andrea, Mr. Carter. I don't like to be called 'doctor.' I'm not a veterinarian."

"As long as you call me Paul, as in Paul Rainsford. That's what I'll be from now on."

She nodded, and I closed the door behind me. I went to her workbench and peered into the large, plastic pan. In it, two long pieces of flint were propped up on an improvised stage of toothpicks and jar tops. "A flint tool," I said, "for scraping, isn't it?"

"Very good," she replied. "I see you've done your homework. This *is* a flint working tool. I'm preparing to make a mold of it. It came from the same section of Man-

churia to which we'll be going. Do you know what's significant about it?''

I said that I didn't.

"It's identical to a flint scraper that was found in 1936 in
the La Brea Tar Pits . . .''

"California?''

"Yes, and dated in 1972 as being 23,600 years old. If
indeed the Manchurian scraper is identical to the one an early
American used to scrape the flesh off the bones of a dwarf
mammoth . . .''

"It gives us an idea where the first Americans came
from,'' I finished her sentence.

She nodded. "It has always been accepted that the American Indians came from East Asia, but exactly where has
never been known. Now we have the chance to know. We'll
go to the Kumara site and see if we can't find out.''

"What's there now?''

"A good-sized bone pit with datable strata. How much of
this do you want to know, Dr. Rainsford?''

"Paul,'' I corrected.

"Whatever.''

"I want to know the lay of the land and how many people
will be peeking over our shoulders,'' I said.

"Have a seat,'' she said, waving a hand in the direction of
a plain, gray metal desk atop which sat numerous piles of
papers.

Andrea sat behind the desk and fiddled with one of the
piles of paper big enough to produce a thickly-stuffed manila
envelope. She spilled the contents onto her blotter and sifted
through it.

"I don't have pictures of the site, but I've got a fairly good
description from Peking. It's thickly forested, with rolling
hills and a few small peaks. The dig is in a river valley, far
from any regular habitation. There is a nomadic tribe which
ranges seasonally through the area, but no settlements and
only a dirt road.''

"How did the dirt road get there?'' I asked.

"My impression is that it was a military reconnaissance route in use during the border skirmishes of the 1960s. I'm told that it's no longer in use."

Sure, I thought.

"The dig is seven miles from Kumara and two miles from the border. It's absolutely isolated. That seems to be important to you."

"If it's so isolated," I asked, "how come we know about it?"

"The usual way. A native from the nomadic tribe I mentioned walked into Kumara and sold a trinket he carved out of bone. A soldier bought it and, on leave in Peking, showed it to his father-in-law, who is a professor of archaeology and recognized the bone as having come from a mammoth. *That's* how the site was discovered."

The explanation was plausible enough. "How far is the site from the dirt road?"

"Several hundred yards. The road parallels the river for quite a distance."

"Okay. Now, who will be going?"

"Myself, three research associates and you. In China we'll pick up a jeep driver and four retainers. And you will have an assistant, I think."

"Apparently," I said, still harboring no great love of the notion.

"Here is all my information about the locale. Why *will* you be joining us, Dr. Rainsford?"

"Do you really want to know that?"

"No, I don't suppose I do. I won't pretend I like the idea of your going along."

"You like the idea of our picking up the tab for the expedition, don't you? Not to mention a sizable chunk of the museum's annual operating expenses."

Her temper flared, and she drummed her fingers angrily on the blotter. "We could do it without you."

"You could run the museum without us, maybe, but

mount million-dollar expeditions to the wilds of Manchuria? Be serious for a minute."

"I don't like working for the military," she hissed.

"We're an intelligence agency, not a branch of the military. Look, most of the research into solar energy is being funded by NASA, and all of it involves defense. What the hell makes you so different? We're getting a good cover story, and you're getting to run around the world picking up whatever bones suit your fancy."

Andrea said no more, but her fingers continued their drumming.

"Do you imagine you would be let into a border area of communist China without the Chinese getting more out of it than the satisfaction of making a contribution to science?"

"Okay," she sighed, "I give up. I won't say another word, but I still don't intend to like it."

"You like to eat, don't you?"

"What?" she asked.

"How about dinner tonight?" I asked.

"No, Mr. Carter," she said with a scornful laugh. "I don't think I have time to have dinner with you this evening."

I was unconvinced by her rejection. She seemed nervous, and I don't think it had anything to do with working with AXE.

I had the clear impression that despite her attempts to hide it, her sensuality was aching to be let loose. A few seconds later, I had occasion to wonder if I wasn't wrong.

"Oyster Bar, the Plaza, seven-thirty."

"I have to go to Manchuria with you," she snapped. "I don't have to like you. Now, if you have everything you came for . . ."

I shrugged, said goodbye, and left. This would not be the end of it. Nothing worthwhile comes easy.

I dined alone at the Oyster Bar, having a huge steak, baked

potatoes and, of course, oysters. It was an agreeable businessman's bar, and not too busy to prevent my having a leisurely meal. Halfway through coffee, Andrea showed up and helped herself to a seat. She had changed from the jeans she wore at the museum to a conservative linen suit. Even when going out, she maintained a high level of decorum. I sensed that swallowing her pride and meeting me was not the simplest thing she had ever done. A compromise was to arrive late.

"I was wondering if you'd still be here," she said.

"Would you like something to eat?"

"No thanks. I had a bite after the symposium."

"Symposium?" I asked.

"At NYU. It's a regular monthly thing. It meant I couldn't meet you as you asked. Look, I'm sorry I snapped at you this afternoon."

"Forget it."

"I realize you have a job to do like everyone else."

I tossed my hands up. There was nothing I could tell her.

"When we get to Manchuria, will you have to . . . I mean . . ."

"You don't want to know," I said softly.

"Can't you tell me anything?"

"I . . . have to go out in the woods for a few days. That's all. Nothing you would consider dramatic."

"Okay," she said softly, thought a moment, then said idly, "I like the woods myself. I was raised upstate, in the Adirondacks. My father was a park ranger. I like to do things like hike and backpack. There hasn't been much time lately. I've been so busy."

"There will be plenty of chances where we're going."

She smiled then, and I thought I had broken through to her. But there was an interruption, a rustling of fabric as a newcomer pushed through the roomful of diners, and Rita Brennan presented herself. It couldn't have happened at a worse moment. Just as I was getting Andrea to open up to me.

"Hi," Rita said brightly, bending over to kiss me on the forehead. Andrea paled, and I could see her retreating back into her shell. As always, Rita looked spectacular and showed no reluctance in showing off her assets. I made the introductions.

"Paul saved my life last night," Rita said.

"Oh," Andrea replied, coolly.

"There were two muggers. I was lucky. I didn't expect to see you tonight, Rita."

"I've been looking for you all afternoon. The message desk said you were down here. I hope you don't mind my dropping in. Have I interrupted something?"

"Not at all," Andrea said stiffly, getting to her feet and nearly upsetting her chair at the same time. "Dr. Rainsford and I were having a professional discussion."

"Which we must continue very soon," I replied, jumping to my feet just as quickly. It did no good. Andrea smiled sweetly, said goodbye, and was gone. When she was out of sight, I turned on Rita, who had a conqueror's look about her.

"Not very good timing, Rita," I said, trying to look annoyed. "You'll pay dearly for this tonight "

FIVE

"What do you mean?" she protested. "Was that something serious?"

"If it was, it sure isn't now," I replied.

"Oh, I'm *sorry,*" she said, meaning it not a bit. "I *will* make it up to you. I have already, in fact. I did your room."

"You did what to my room?"

"Fixed it up. You're not much of a housekeeper, Paul."

"God invented maids for that purpose. How did you get into my room?"

"Simple. I told the desk clerk I was your wife. Come on up and see what I did."

Rita Brennan seemed fully prepared and quite capable of wheedling her way into my life; taking it over, if that was possible, which it wasn't. I was intrigued by her. If she was setting me up, it was the most bald-faced attempt I could imagine. I finished my coffee, paid the bill and left with her draped on my arm.

My suite had been thoroughly cleaned up and adorned with a vase of fresh flowers in both main rooms. The suit I wore on the flight from Edinburgh was cleaned and pressed, and the

27

pair of hiking boots left in the closet were polished. A platter of fresh fruit and cheeses sat on the table next to chilled vodka and a fifth of my brand of scotch. Rita must have been through everything in the suite. Of course, nothing in it indicated my real name or made mention of AXE.

"This must have taken hours," I speculated.

"Three."

"Do you ever work? Most people can't afford to take off three hours in the afternoon."

"Hey. I'm an important person. After my coverage of the Iran-Iraq War, I can pretty much write my own ticket. Taking a couple of hours off is no problem. How was your day?"

"Fair," I said, pouring us drinks.

"What happened in your meeting this morning?"

"The usual. I learned about a new dig which has some promise."

"Oh? Tell me about it."

"You're not interested in archaeology," I said.

"Who says? Where is this 'dig'?"

"In China."

"China, as in communist China?"

"That's the place. Manchuria, to be exact. My colleagues think they have a handle on the origins of the original human settlers of the Americas. We're mounting an expedition. It leaves in a few days."

"When exactly?" she asked, a calculating look in her eye.

"Tuesday."

"I can be ready by then."

"What?"

"I'm going with you, of course."

"Don't be ridiculous."

"You'll need a photographer. Someone to shoot the artifacts before they're excavated. I know how it's done."

I had a belt of scotch and said, patiently, "I don't have the budget for another hand. I'd really love to run around the Manchurian wilds with you, but . . ."

"*I* have the budget. I told you I can write my own ticket. Sure, there are some approvals involved, but I can get by them."

"Rita . . ."

"No arguments! Think of what an assignment in Manchuria would mean to my career. Most of the photographers the Chinese have let in have been restricted to Peking and the industrial areas. Wouldn't it be wonderful if I could get some shots of the northern countryside?"

"Terrific."

"I assume the Chinese will give me a visa," she said.

"At this point," I replied, "I don't see how anyone can deny you anything."

"Then it's okay with you that I go along?"

In reply I set down my glass and hers, took her blouse in both my hands and from the bottom I ripped up. The buttons popped off in sequence exposing her scant bra underneath. She sucked in her breath. Instead of searching for a clasp to fumble with, I grabbed the front of her bra between her cleavage and neatly tore it off exposing her large, magnificent breasts. "I said you'd have to pay for what you did before."

"No man has ever done that to me," she gasped.

"Stick around," I said, and went to her.

The smell of Hawk's cigar cleared one section of the Oyster Bar's bar. We stood alone, with the half-dozen other patrons huddled at the other end of the bar.

"She checks out clean," Hawk said, tipping some ashes into a wooden bowl that he had just cleared of pretzels.

"I thought she would," I replied.

"If Rita Brennan is anything but what she says she is, we can't prove it. She has been a faithful employee of UANS for several years, and has, in fact, been nominated for a Pulitzer for her coverage of the Iran-Iraq war. To put it short, Nick, she's—"

"Just another crazy lady like all the women I seem to attract," I cut in.

"It kind of looks that way. Do you really want to take her to Manchuria with you?"

"Why not? If she's really just a photographer, there will be no harm in it. If she's more than that, I'd like to know. If she's setting me up, I'd like to keep her close by."

"That sounds reasonable. I can get the visa for her with no trouble. Obviously, she'll have to pay for herself. You're an academic, remember, and don't have the money to take strange women halfway around the world."

I nodded. "And having a legitimate news photographer on hand will help us in case the Russians get wind of the expedition. They may think it really *is* just an archaeological dig."

"You hope," Hawk said.

"Yes, sir, I do."

"Okay, Nick," he said, "take her with you. Use the expected precautions, and sit with your back to the wall. Your money is in your Washington account. You'll fly to San Francisco on Tuesday, and the freighter sails the day after. I never knew scientists carried so much junk with them."

"Two and a half tons," I said.

"Have a nice time in Manchuria," Hawk said and, with a comradely pat on the upper arm, was gone.

When I got back to my suite, Rita was lying in bed asleep. The television was on, and buzzing away. I undressed, slid into bed beside her and lit a cigarette. She stirred as my skin touched hers.

"*Umf*," she said.

"Go back to sleep," I replied.

"Where were you?"

"Out."

"There's another woman. I knew it. My mother warned me about men like you." She didn't sound too convincing.

"You can come to Manchuria with me. But you have to

pay your own way. I'm afraid we scientists fall into the ranks with the poor.''

Rita turned toward me, smiled through sleepy eyes and rested her hand on my groin. "I pay for everything I do," she said.

SIX

The figure of the man was crudely drawn, with thick, exaggerated features meant to portray the impression of a thug given in 1930s gangster movies. He held a revolver in his hand, a Smith & Wesson six-shooter with a snub nose pointed right at me. I held the Luger upright, its barrel nearly touching my forehead; breathed in and out, leveled the automatic at the target and left a neat circle of eight 9mm holes in the man's chest.

"Very good, Mr. Carter," said the white-robed AXE technician as he took Wilhelmina from me, extracted the spent magazine and inserted a full one. "You get better all the time."

"Thanks," I smiled, and slipped the Luger into its holster.

"Everything you need is built into pockets in your pack—five hundred rounds of ammunition, an extra stiletto, and an extra gas bomb. It's all in the lining. No one will find it but you."

"Who will be looking in an archaeologist's backpack for ammunition, anyway?" I questioned, knowing that where I was going, lots of people might.

"It's three o'clock, sir. Your ship leaves in two hours."

I shook the technician's hand and found my way out of the Fort Scott shooting range. The midafternoon sunlight was dazzling in the Presidio, glinting off the massive steel cables of the Golden Gate. Soon I would be looking at that edifice from quite another angle. I let myself into my Avis Dodge and turned the key in the ignition.

I drove east on Mason past the Crissy Field railroad yard and, leaving the Palace of Fine Arts to my right, entered Marina Boulevard. Traffic was heavy as I drove down Bay Street past Ghirardelli Square, picking up the Embarcadero at Pier 33. It took nearly an hour to find the Avis car drop near Embarcadero Station. Then, struck by an impulse that was highly ironic considering where I was going, I walked up Pine in search of Chinese food.

There was a small takeout restaurant at the corner of Clay and Kearny, right on the outskirts of Chinatown. I placed an order for prawns in hot garlic sauce to go, and looked idly out the window while it was being prepared.

I saw her immediately. Andrea Regan, her cloud of honey blonde hair unmistakable even in the shade across Kearny, was enmeshed in conversation with a young Oriental. A dingy import-export firm had a windowful of cheap Chinese and Japanese toys. They stood in the doorway, the man doing most of the talking, while Andrea looked around nervously. The Oriental was in his twenties and wore cheap cotton pants and basketball sneakers. She stuck her hands in the pockets of her jeans, then pulled one out and pressed something into the man's hand.

"I'll be back," I told the cashier, and left the restaurant.

Andrea went around the corner and disappeared down Clay in the direction of the wharf. I crossed the street toward the man. He saw me, shot glances quickly in both directions, then took off at a run. He ran north on Kearny with me half a block behind, swung left on Washington and sped west into the heart of Chinatown. He was fast and wore sneakers. I was fast too, but wearing dress Oxfords was no match for him. He lost me in the teeming mass of Orientals filling the streets, sidewalks, and shops at the intersection of Washington and Grant. The fortunes of war, I thought, and walked back to the restaurant to pick up my order.

Twenty minutes later, I sat on a mooring post on the fantail of the S.S. *Rainwater,* eating prawns that were but slightly cooled by the walk from Chinatown to the wharf. The California class steamship was not large but it was new, with accomodations for twelve paying passengers that included large staterooms facing forward, a dining room and library. The expedition's equipment was long since stowed, and members were at the beginning of a long period where they would have nothing to do. I was looking forward to it; my three days off in New York was far too brief, and I needed the rest. I also needed more time to wonder what the hell was the meaning of Andrea's afternoon meeting with the Oriental man on the outskirts of Chinatown. At least, I thought, she didn't know I was aware of it.

As if I had just called her, Andrea appeared. She had avoided me since that evening in New York when Rita broke up what otherwise could have been a terrific relationship. She appeared nervous, like she was on the street corner, and I wondered if she hadn't noticed me after all.

"Hi," she said, a bit stiffly.

"Afternoon. Would you like a bite?"

"No thanks. I'm looking forward to finding out what the food is like aboard ship."

"It's your funeral. I've had freighter food, and knew enough to pick up some Chinese before we sailed."

"Where'd you get it?" she asked, with no apparent interest.

"A little joint at Clay and Kearny."

If Andrea was uptight about my recently having been at the site of her meeting, she didn't show it. Neither did she mention having been there. The puzzle remained.

"When you get a chance," she said, "I'd like you to have a look at the Land Rover. I don't know if it's tied down right."

"Sure thing. Look, since you *are* having dinner tonight, do you think we might try again?"

"What, and disappoint Rita?"

That time her emotion was quite clear.

"Rita is a big girl. She can eat by herself."

"Did you *have* to bring her along? I realize I'm intruding into your personal life, but . . ."

"My personal life, such as it is, has almost nothing to do with it. She's a good photographer, and her presence there will free one of your research associates to dig. Besides, she's paying her own way, and her printing photos of the expedition will quite conceivably result in more funding for the museum. Do you want more reasons?"

Andrea nodded begrudgingly. "Does she know who you really are?"

"She had better not," I said.

"Okay, Dr. Rainsford . . ."

"Paul," I corrected.

"Okay, Paul, I'll have dinner with you. But only if you do as I ask and check the Land Rover."

"Consider it done," I replied, stuffing my empty food carton bag in its sack and crushing the whole thing for deposit in the nearest can.

There was a blast on the ship's horn, and deckhands began moving about the fantail, tugging on the mammoth, six-inch-thick lines. I went below to do as I had been asked.

At dinner I had soup and a small green salad while Andrea enjoyed what appeared to be, to my surprise, a genuinely good meal of sautéed bass with almond slivers. The S.S. *Rainwater* took her lines in and backed out of her wharf just a few minutes late, rounded the north end of the San Francisco peninsula and within minutes was in the shadow of the

Golden Gate. As that spiderweb of steel and concrete passed above and behind us, we wandered out onto the observation deck. We were sailing straight into the sun, which made looking aft a necessary pleasure. Andrea sat on her deck chair, quietly sipping her Benedictine, while the coastline of America slipped away.

All through dinner, we had discussed nothing but archaeology. She regaled me with all the information at her disposal about the origins of the first Americans, the similarities between American Indians and certain Tartar groups, and the like. This was a conversation I could keep up with. I knew the basic theories of how early man walked from Siberia to Alaska across a "bridge" formed during two ice ages when sea levels were down enough to expose what is now the bottom of the Bering Strait. The tribes followed the caribou herds south through the Yukon Territory, arriving about twenty-five thousand years ago in what is now the continental United States, spreading quickly through North and South America. The conversation was enlightening for more than the obvious reason: Andrea was trying to say something without saying it. I was certain she was attracted to me, but could not express it. Her womanhood, I felt, had long been dormant, a common enough if lamentable condition among brainy women. Her spectacular figure would have added to her dilemma by making her the object of cheap advances practically from the moment of puberty. These could be the reasons she was keeping her distance. Then again, there was the Oriental man she met in San Francisco. As the freighter pulled out of sight of the American mainland at last, I was acutely aware of being surrounded by puzzling women.

"We'll be in Shanghai before long," I said.

Andrea nodded, took a sip of brandy and rested her glass on the deck. She sighed, braced herself and asked, "Do you kill people?"

"So that's it."

"That's part of it. Do you?"

"Will you believe me if I say 'no'?"

She shook her head.

"Then you have your answer."

Andrea took back her glass and, this time, drained it.

"I'm afraid of you," she said.

"You're a good deal more than that."

"Do you *like* killing people? I mean, is it fun?"

"If you were a survivor of Auschwitz, would you enjoy killing your Nazi guard?" I asked.

"The comparison is hardly apt in the 1980s."

"Isn't it?" I laughed. "Have you been paying any attention to what's going on in Uganda . . . Cambodia . . . Afghanistan? Have you been paying *real* attention? I mean, can you see the actual blood and guts, not just the clinical reports?"

"I haven't been to any of those places."

"You ought to go. It's very enlightening. There are horrible things going on all over the world. I do what I can. If it makes you feel any better, my reason for going to Manchuria has nothing to do with taking lives, although it may happen if things get rough. What I'm after will save lives. Lots of lives. I can't tell you more than that. You'll have to take my word for it."

She was silent for quite a while, then said, with a vague sort of resignation, "I've never met anyone quite like you."

"There are damn few of us left," I replied.

"There was a time when I would celebrate that fact. Now, I'm not so sure. You confuse as well as frighten me. I thought all people in your line of work were rednecks. It's disconcerting to find they're not. I'm sorry, Paul, but it's going to take a lot of thinking before I can understand you."

"You think too much already."

"I've been accused of it. Look, I think I'd better go."

She stood, stuck her hands in her pockets, which I now realized was a nervous gesture, and said, "We'll talk again."

"Stay," I said, but she ignored me and rushed off.

I watched her go, then finished my own drink and lay back in the soft webbing of the deck chair until sleep swept over me.

SEVEN

The first evening aboard the S.S. *Rainwater* was a beautiful one, even if Andrea seemed to have disappeared altogether. I found a comfortable chair in the library, smoked a few cigarettes and read the San Francisco papers, the last up-to-date American papers I would see for some time. At eleven I went to the bar and watched the news on television, the signal fading with each mile we made to sea. Rita was spending the evening as she spent the afternoon—taking roll after roll of photos of the ship, the crew, the ocean. I was bored. There was nothing to do but go to sleep.

I went out on deck first. The sea breeze was cool and brisk, and caused the rigging to flap against the three tall cargo booms mounted fore of the bridge. The sound reminded me of sailing boats I had known, and I meant to enjoy it.

The forecastle was a short six steps up from the main cargo deck, reachable by port and starboard ladders. I climbed one of them and walked up the forecastle toward the bow. Two of the cargo booms were mounted on that foremost deck. When I cleared the stanchion supporting the one nearest the bow, I found where Andrea had been hiding.

She stood at the peak of the bow, looking out to sea ahead of the ship, her long hair whipping behind her. There was something different about the way she dressed this time. She wore the same faded jeans as before and a red plaid flannel shirt. But the shirt was tied beneath her breasts, exposing her middle, and she wore no bra. Even through the thick flannel, her nipples could be seen, erect and straining the fabric. I was certain she had been waiting for me to find her.

"So this is where you've been."

She wheeled toward me, slightly surprised by the sound, then smiled. "It's so lovely up here," she said.

I moved up behind her and slipped my arm around her waist. She stiffened when my fingers touched her bare skin, then relaxed and rested her head on my shoulder.

"I was hoping you'd come looking for me," she said after a minute.

I hadn't precisely gone looking for her, but wasn't about to spoil the illusion. "I scoured the ship," I told her. There are many times when a lie is charitable.

She twisted to face me, and the wind now blew her hair into a corolla around her face. I framed her face with my hands, pushing the hair to the sides, and drew her to me. Our lips met, and with a whimper she gave in. Her arms went around my waist and pulled me to her until our hips touched, hers moving ever so slightly against mine.

Andrea clung to me with as much desperation as desire, her tongue battling fiercely with mine. She didn't seduce easily, I realized, but when she did it was one hell of a show. As I thought about her when we first met, nothing worthwhile comes easy.

Suddenly, she pulled away. "I . . . I don't know what this means," she gasped.

"Don't worry about what it means. Enjoy how it feels."

"I . . ."

"Stop thinking with your head."

"What?" she asked, astonished.

"Let another part of your body be your guide." And I pulled open the knot holding the halves of her blouse together. Her breasts spilled out into the night air; she sucked in her breath as I grasped them in both my hands, feeling the nipples against my palms. She ground her hips against me again and moaned as she felt me swell.

She was looking over my shoulder; there was an instant where she tensed, frightened, and it had nothing to do with sex. Andrea had seen something that scared the hell out of her.

"Paul!" she yelled, in a panic-stricken voice.

She yanked at my shoulders and in doing so, pulled me down. There was the roar of a revolver and a bullet took a chunk of paint off the rail where my back had just been.

"Stay down!" I barked at Andrea.

I shoved her to the deck and at the same time I rolled in the direction of my assailant, pulling Wilhelmina from her holster and yanking on the bolt.

Andrea crawled behind a mooring post and stayed there, curled into a frightened ball, tugging incongruously at the loose halves of her blouse, as if modesty mattered at the moment.

There was movement behind the first cargo boom, a flash of fire, and two more slugs. When they had spent their energy at sea I jumped up, fired one round in the direction of the boom, and dived to my right. I skirted the port foreward lifeboat and when I emerged from behind it, saw the figure of a man running aft. I fired another shot at him. He faltered, spun and clicked off two more shots. He had fired five so far which meant there should be only two left. A revolver has a different sound from an automatic, and no revolvers have more than seven shots.

He was moving again, heading for the starboard ladder which led down to the main cargo deck. "Go to my cabin and wait," I yelled to Andrea, then took off after him.

There was a bottleneck by the starboard ladder: a jumble of

mooring lines not yet stowed. He didn't judge them correctly and stumbled and fell. He rolled, fired a shot which came nowhere near me, then scrambled to his feet. He was wearing all black. I had him squarely in my sights from a distance of ten yards. As he got to his feet, the hand with the gun started to come up.

"Don't even think about it," I said.

The hand fell back down, and his shoulders slumped.

"Come into the light where I can see you."

He didn't do it. He stepped backward to the rail until his back was pressed against it.

"Identify yourself," I said.

He said nothing and didn't move. His head was perfectly outlined against the moonlit sky. I stepped closer, keeping my automatic trained on him. When I was close enough for him to see it, I said, "I'm going to give you one chance to explain yourself. One chance."

He shook his head. I fired a shot which singed the hair on the right side of his head. The man cringed, then straightened.

"Start talking, and make the story good. You just interrupted a beautiful evening, and I'm not in the mood to listen to tall tales."

He seemed to be crying and shook his head again. I took aim at the left side of his head and fired another round. It missed his left ear by millimeters.

"Don't make me kill you. Tell me who you are."

He slumped a bit, kept his silence and seemed to be gathering his strength. He straightened then, raised his hand, and I saw the glint of moonlight off his gun barrel.

"Damn," I swore, and pulled the trigger.

I hit him in the center of the forehead and tore the top of his head off. My 9mm bullet expanded on impact, blowing the man's brain out the fist-sized hole it made in the back of his head, spraying the sea with gray. His body flipped backwards after it, folding over the rail and slipping into the ocean, leaving not a trace on the deck.

I stood for a moment, wondering what the hell was going on and which of the two women he was hooked up with. Then lights began to flick on around the bridge, and I heard the murmur of frightened voices. I went below before anyone could see me. Andrea was in my stateroom, pacing the floor nervously. I took her in my arms. "What's *happening*?" she asked almost hysterical.

"I caught him. An Oriental, probably Chinese, in his thirties, I think. I had to kill him."

"Oh, my God."

"He went over the side without a trace. It will be interesting to see if he's listed on the crew roster."

"Paul . . . Jesus, what's going *on* here? That man was trying to kill you!"

"I don't know that. He could have been trying to kill *you*. Or us. Who knows? He preferred to die rather than talk."

She broke away from me, looked down at the floor and said, "Everything's happening so fast. I just don't understand."

I held her again, until she calmed down. "Don't worry," I said. "Just trust me."

Andrea said nothing, but hugged me as hard as she could. She was still for a long time, scarcely breathing, and then she erupted in passion. Andrea pulled at me, tearing at my clothes, undressing me as I undressed her. I guided her to the bed and she took me into her, crying out loud and thrashing her head from side to side. When she climaxed, it was in a great storm of voice and muscles and sweat and was followed by a long calm where nothing was said. I sensed her pulling back into her shell and knew that, for the time, there was nothing I could do to prevent it. Then slowly she started to dress.

"Stay with me tonight," I said. "We'll have breakfast sent in."

She was irritable. "I don't know what came over me.

There's just something about you, that's all. And the situation . . . the ship, the moonlight, and your having saved me."

"As I recall, *you* saved *me*."

"Paul . . . Dr. Rainsford . . . We have to spend a long time together, and—"

I waved my hand as if to erase the entire line of thought. "If you don't want to stay here tonight, I won't force you. If you don't want to sleep with me again, I won't scream and yell. I don't want you to isolate yourself from me, but if I can't prevent it, then I'll accept it. Most of all, I don't want to see you get shot at simply because you're with me. If keeping your distance keeps you out of danger, I'll understand. I would never want to endanger you."

Andrea seemed to calm down and, fumbling with the knot which held her blouse tied, let me do it for her.

"There," I said, finishing, "your dignity is preserved. You can go now. But I wish you wouldn't."

Andrea relaxed then, hugged me, and kissed me on the lips.

"I like you," she said. "But I can't accept what you do for a living. I'm a scientist, not a spy. I don't like getting shot at. Please keep me out of it from now on."

And, with a slam of my door, she was gone.

EIGHT

Our arrival in Shanghai provoked little apparent interest among the Chinese. It was the beginning of another torrid summer. There were fish to be caught, ships to be loaded and children to be raised. The spectre of a handful of Americans come to dig up bones seemed to interest no one. That was fine with me. There had been enough excitement aboard ship. After the gun battle on the foredeck, the captain nearly tore up the ship trying to figure out what the hell had happened. I didn't volunteer any information and, the dead man being an apparent stowaway, the captain was left with nothing.

There was a two-day layover in Shanghai while the expedition's equipment was transferred from the *Rainwater* to a small, Chinese coastal freighter for the short hop north to Tientsin. I was glad for the shore leave. After the initial excitement, the trip had become a bit boring. Andrea avoided me, keeping to her books and lording over the scientific equipment as if it were made out of gold. But Rita Brennan finished her shipboard picture-taking almost immediately, and made the long nights at sea at least bearable.

The dockside scene by the mouth of the Yangtse was

typically chaotic. Unlike the center of the Chinese mainland, the old dock to which the *Rainwater* was moored looked like the communist revolution had never occurred. While longshoremen wore the usual green uniforms, the clothes were tattered and dirty, patched here and there with rags which also saw service as sweatbands. The pier was filthy with oil drums, rust and dry rot, and smelled of long, hard and generally disrespectful use. Rita loved it, ignoring the stares of the men as she bounced all over the place, snapping pictures once again.

"Hey, where do we go now?" Rita finally asked. "I have to cable my wire service and tell them I landed."

"The American trade mission is a few blocks from here. I'll drop you off, then run an errand of my own. Later on, we'll meet and see if we can scare up some iced tea."

Rita took my arm and we walked up the pier toward the main harbor road, looking for all the world like more of the American tourists who had begun to flood the mainland. Her camera was repeatedly at her eye, the automatic winder clicking off stops as Rita found memorable hand carts, fish stands and narrow streets of the ancient city. A pudgy prostitute wearing a once-elegant red dress reminded me of the one in New York; she leaned in a manner she thought was seductive in the unused back door of a small shop selling candles and fabric. The woman scanned us briefly, gave Rita a vicious glance, then looked in another direction.

The Trade Mission was as I remembered it, a square, modern building of sand-colored stone which, although just four stories tall, dominated the intersection upon which it sat. On the ground level was a service area where American nationals could cash checks, send cables home, get travel advice or hire the services of a translator. Behind the cable desk was a young Chinese, a girl not out of her teens, who spoke passable English. I left Rita with her, agreeing to meet back at the ship in an hour.

Once back on the street, I returned to the harbor road,

walking north toward that part of the old city where the shoreline curved inland with the Yangtse. Half a dozen blocks of crates, cargo booms and jabbering longshoremen went by before I found the large, old storefront shipping office marked by the legend Propylon Trading Company. Behind a dirt-streaked window, three Chinese clerks occupied old mahogany desks while a large ceiling fan turned languidly.

I pushed my way inside and said to the first one who looked at me, "Mr. Pendle, please."

The clerk was a rather unattractive middle-aged woman, as were the other workers in the front office of Propylon.

"Who is asking?"

"Paul Rainsford. He's expecting me."

She nodded and shuffled off, her sandles, cut from old auto tires, making clopping noises on the wood floor.

The office hadn't changed a bit in the three years since I last came to Shanghai. A vintage Marilyn Monroe calendar shared a wall with a collection of license plates going back to 1927; another wall had a gigantic map detailing steamer routes throughout the Pacific. I felt as if I was on the set of a Bogart movie, and that the man I had come to see was not Arthur Pendle, but Sidney Greenstreet.

But it was Pendle who beckoned to me from the door to his back office.

"Professor Rainwater! Come in, come in."

The Chinese clerk opened the gate which was the only way to get past the waist-high office divider other than vaulting it, and I walked through. Pendle grasped my hand and, once we were behind the closed door of his inner office, said "Good to see you again, Nick. How have you been?"

"Fair. And yourself?"

"The same as always. I hear you had luck in Scotland."

"It was bloody, but interesting," I replied.

"You never do get bored, do you? I envy you that."

"Your life is a lot safer."

"I suppose it is." he sighed, and indicated for me to sit down.

Actually, Pendle's life was rather unsafe, and it had been that way for nearly forty years. A British national, Pendle was His Majesty's operative in Shanghai at the end of World War II, and stayed on after the revolution to work for AXE as well as MI5. His cover was the import-export company which while shabby was profitable enough for all concerned so that the Mao regime tolerated it.

Pendle was a nearly-bald man, a bit thick around the middle, but with a ruddy complexion and a strength undiminished by his fifty-eight years. We had worked together many times; most notably on a bloody mission which had us preventing the Chinese from sabotaging a Japanese-American ocean-bottom mining venture in the South China Sea. That one got very messy, but as always Pendle came away clean. He was the idea man, the arranger. He never went into battle and never blew his cover. As a result, he was always there to help us when we needed it. Several generations of AXE men had their skins saved by him one way or the other.

"Hawk sent this for you," Pendle said, and pushed across his old, oaken desk a pack of my custom-blend cigarettes. I hadn't brought any with me for the usual reason: it's hard for a man whose initials are supposed to be PR to explain why he has the letters NC embossed in gold on his filter tips.

"I appreciate it," I said, lighting one and blowing smoke casually across the century-old desk which Pendle swore (but no one believed) came from one of the old China tea clippers.

"So we're working *with* the Chinese this time, are we?" Pendle remarked with a sardonic smile.

"So I hear."

"For once," he said, the smile replaced by an unmistakable tone of foreboding, "I'm rather glad I'm not going along."

NINE

"I'm sure you are," I replied, with sarcasm to match his own.

"Let's just say that you can have this one all to yourself, Nick. I hear it's been a real delight already."

"The two guys in New York."

"About whom we still know nothing. I was referring also to the Oriental you chased around San Francisco, about whom we also know nothing."

"I was hoping the department would have *some* lead on the man," I said.

"Not a damn thing, I'm sorry to say. We have run a preliminary check on your friend with the large, uh, chest, but it's come up zero so far."

"A model citizen, huh?"

"It would appear that way. From a cursory examination of her record, she has no blemishes. We'll go into it in depth, of course, if you think it worthwhile."

I thought for a moment. "I'm not sure about her. She's a complicated woman with a lot of doubts. If she's putting on an act, it's a damn good one. And she did save my life."

51

"I beg your pardon," Pendle said, arching an eyebrow.

"I was with her on the foredeck when someone took a shot at us—"

"I did intercept a radio message from your captain reporting what sounded like a gun battle," Pendle cut in, "but he went on to say there was no one hurt or missing and neither crew nor passengers volunteered information. I thought you might have had a hand in it. Who was the man?"

"Another Oriental in his twenties. I got a good look at his face before I had to shoot it off. He might have been Chinese, with maybe a bit more of the classic Mongoloid look than usual."

"Maybe Manchurian or Korean?"

"Or Siberian," I said, making sure Pendle knew I thought the possibility significant.

He pondered the notion for a moment, then asked, "Who do you think he was shooting at? The lady or yourself?"

"I'm the obvious choice," I replied, "but maybe you had better dig a little deeper into her past."

"Consider it done," Pendle responded, scribbling a note on a scratch pad which carried the logo of a Hong Kong tailor.

"Anyway, the guy went over the side when I blew his head off, so there's no positive way of telling what the hell was going on."

Pendle nodded, then shrugged. Some things couldn't be helped.

"I think he knew he was going to die," I went on. "I mean, he might have even committed suicide. I told him not to raise his gun and he did anyway."

"Zealots abound in this part of the world," Pendle said idly.

I stood, stretched and gazed at one of Pendle's wall decorations—a collage of photos of post-war Shanghai—while he finished his scribbling.

"Do you need any more munitions to replace those lost?" he asked finally.

"Another box of 9mm will do."

He noted it, then stood and took my hand. "Your stuff should be on the coastal freighter by tomorrow morning," he said. "She's a small ship, and rather ancient, but reliable. They call her the Shan Yang."

"The Goat," I said with a smile.

"I thought you might find that amusing. At any rate, it's a short journey to Tientsin, so you'll be safe enough on the Shan Yang. Try not to get yourself killed all the same."

"I'll do my best."

"As for your Chinese 'guide,' my information is that you'll be contacted in Tientsin. I know nothing about who it will be."

"Hmm," I said.

"They appear to be especially secretive on this one," Pendle went on. "As you know, they're desperate to keep their names out of it, in case the whole thing falls through and a shooting war develops with the Russians. I'll be riding up to Tientsin with you. I have an office there, and the cover of having made the freight arrangements for the expedition. I'll find out what I can about the man once he's contacted you."

"I know what I have to do," I said, walking to the back window and looking out. The view showed a narrow side-street, but at an oblique angle which let me see a hundred yards down the road. It was little-trafficked, but had a few shops and restaurants of interest and, in front of one, Andrea stood talking with a young Chinese.

"This is getting to be a habit," I said.

"What?" Pendle asked, joining me.

"That's Andrea."

He scrutinized her, then said, "I always did admire a woman with a sturdy frame. What do you suppose she's doing there?"

"I'll let you know when I find out," I replied, and went after her.

By the time I had gotten out of Pendle's office and back into the alley, Andrea had left the company of her newest

Oriental acquaintance and was walking slowly north, away from the waterfront, looking in shop windows.

The young man with whom she spoke was nowhere to be seen, and I didn't waste time looking. If I could lose an Oriental in Chinatown, there would be no hope of tracking one in Shanghai. Keeping out of sight, I followed Andrea instead.

She walked up one street and down another, in no apparent direction, looking in all the windows and in general behaving like a typical tourist. As she progressed further and further into the oldest part of the city, Andrea appeared to have no knowledge of the danger around her. The streets were narrower, so slender and cramped that except at high noon no sunlight could penetrate them. The shops were old and indescribably dingy. I sensed that Peking's "new order" had never heard of them.

Deep into this sinister section of the city, five streets came together in a pentangle. One antiquated tobacco shop, a bare lightbulb shining behind barred windows, was the only sign of life. Andrea halted and looked around, apparently confused. I sensed she had realized just how lost she had become. She checked her watch, then looked back in my direction, but didn't spot me. She sighed, stamped a foot irritably, then turned back my way. It was then that they jumped her.

Three men came out of doorways like the one in which I hid to avoid her, and pounced on her. Two grabbed her arms and the other clamped a gigantic palm over her mouth. A scream was stifled, and the light in the tobacco shop went out.

I stepped out of my hiding place. They dragged her, struggling all the while, into a door which appeared permanently shut but which opened magically when they pressed against it. I ran to it and found it locked. Inside, there was the sound of wooden boxes being knocked over, and an occasional whimper. I drew my automatic, reared back and kicked in the door. It swung open and slammed into the wall, freezing all in the room.

Andrea's blouse had been torn off and her jeans pulled down to her knees. In the crude attempt at gang rape, her panties were slashed off and one man stood behind her, a knife at her neck, while another stood frozen in time, his pants at his ankles, his hand holding a swollen penis. Andrea saw me silhouetted in the light from the doorway, focused through the tears in her eyes and cried out for help.

The man with the erection shook himself out of the ridiculous pose he was in, bent and grabbed for his pants. The one with the knife twisted his head toward me and sneered, as if to threaten. I leveled the Luger at a spot behind his right ear and pulled the trigger once. A small hole appeared in one side of his head as his brains blew out the other. He fell straight down, the knife falling from Andrea's throat to clatter uselessly on the floor.

The third man was behind Andrea, pinning her arms. He was short but muscular, like a wrestler. He let her go, dropped a hand to his belt, and came up with a pistol. In the instant the first man died, the second got off two shots in my direction; both missed high, embedding themselves in the old wood framework above my head.

He aimed a third time. I lowered the sights of Wilhelmina to his chest—the bigger target—and pulled the trigger again and again. It was like target practice on the Fort Scott shooting range in San Francisco. A brace of holes appeared in the man's chest and he was thrown backward, clutching at them as he stumbled over an empty wooden box and fell to the floor, writhing for but a second while life escaped him.

Holstering the Luger, I went toward the last of her attackers. The biggest man, his trousers finally buckled, was waiting for me, his outstretched hands like claws.

"Talk," I said, advancing on him.

He grunted angrily and swung a massive right hand in my direction.

I ducked under the blow and countered with a right to the gut and a sharp left uppercut which caught the point of his jaw and sent the man reeling back against the wall.

"Talk," I repeated, as he pulled himself together.

"I don't understand," he said in Chinese.

"Who are you? Why did you attack her?" I asked in faultless Mandarin.

Startled as well as hurt, the man mumbled, "Pretty girl. No more. No more. Don't hurt me."

I sighed and backed off a step. This would not be easy, or pleasant for Andrea to watch. I would have to wring it out of him and disregard any nonsense about the attack being a simple rape.

But when I backed off, he made a quick motion behind him and, from a cross-beam of the old, wood-frame wall, produced a longshoreman's baling hook and swung it at my head. I jerked back just in time and the pinpoint tip of the hook whizzed past my eyes.

I flicked my wrist and Hugo, my trustworthy stiletto, dropped into my palm from its sheath up my sleeve. I set myself.

The big man took another swipe at me, the hook grazing my shoulder this time.

"Stop or you die," I said in his language.

If he understood, and he must have, he did nothing to save himself. He howled with a samurai's death-charge and went at me, aiming the hook at my neck. I got his neck first. The stiletto sliced his windpipe and jugular neatly and he hung in space for a second, eyes bulging, while blood spurted four feet in front of him. Screaming, Andrea brushed frenziedly at the crimson spots that splattered her breast even as the last of her assailants slid straight down to the floor, as dead as the rest.

TEN

I helped Andrea back into what remained of her blouse, then covered her with my jacket. She held me for a long time, crying and sobbing vaguely intelligible things. When she was calm enough to be moved, I took her to an anteroom that was hardly clean but was at least free of the symptoms of the recent slaughter. I sat her on an old couch and held her until she could speak.

"This is mad. I think I'm mad. You're a bad dream and everything connected with you is the same."

"It must be my mouthwash," I replied.

"Don't make fun, Paul . . . Nick . . . Jesus, I can't even remember which your real name is!"

"Don't let it worry you. You've just been through a hell of an ordeal, and need time to recover."

"About a hundred light years! Why did I get involved in this?"

"Nothing worthwhile comes easy," I said my thoughts returning to when she first rejected me in New York.

"In my entire life, I have not seen so much as a rabbit get run over by a car," she went on. "In the past two weeks, I have been privileged to watch you kill *four people!*"

"At least three of whom were going to rape and/or murder you," I reminded her. "And the intentions of the fourth were pretty dishonorable."

"Agreed," she said with a sigh, slumping down onto the cushions and letting me cuddle her. "I don't mean to seem ungrateful, just perplexed. Why is this happening to me?"

"Just lucky, I guess."

"Paul—"

"You got my name right, anyway. I'm here because I saw those three men following you. I followed the whole bunch of you and, well, here we are. I'm sorry if the volume of blood disturbed you, but killing seldom turns out to be as neat as you'd like it to be. Let's go back to the ship and I'll scrub you down."

She almost smiled. "I can do that myself," she said quickly.

"You're a talented lady," I said.

Andrea laughed, then hugged me back. "I know. Thank you, Paul, or whatever your name is this week. I owe you more than you can imagine. But I really am going to make an effort to stay out of your life, like I told you after that business on the freighter."

"You may not have any choice. Somebody seems intent on linking the two of us."

"Please tell them, that I'm not a player in this drama, nor do I want to become one. I just want to dig my bones and go back to New York."

"Life in the real world ain't that idyllic," I said, giving her a pat on the head and getting to my feet.

"I want it to be," she replied.

"So do I. But until it happens . . ." I walked to the door leading back to the room in which the three bodies lay.

"Where are you going?"

"To see if I can find out who those men are. Or were. I'm getting sick and tired of being shot at by total strangers."

Pendle turned the automatic over and over, poking it with a small screwdriver, grunting now and again as a detail of significance was revealed. Finally, he put it back in my hand.

"It's a fairly standard 9mm Makarov," he said.

"An old one," I added.

"Yes, this gun has seen a few years. If you notice, the trigger-sear linkage is the design the Russians used from 1947 through 1961. The main spring is the old, leaf-type as well."

"The Russians usually send their old equipment to the same place they send their old politicians—Siberia," I said.

"Indeed. During the last border skirmish, the Chinese captured a number of 7.62mm SKS carbines which dated back to the 1930s."

"Which brings us to why a Shanghai thug was using a Russian army pistol."

"Actually, Russian weapons are fairly common here abouts. This old girl—" he patted the Makarov— "may have kicked around the coastline for a couple of decades. On the other hand—"

"It could have been given to its most recent owner for the express purpose of knocking me off," I finished.

"Quite possible."

"A deeper look into Andrea's background is definitely called for," I said.

"And definitely underway. I should have some word by the time you get to Tientsin. I'll also try to trace the gun, but don't hold your breath."

I went to the window from which I saw Andrea a few hours earlier and looked out quietly. "I wonder how she knew I was here," I said.

"She may not have known."

"I'm sure I wasn't followed."

"Miss Regan's appearance on the street may have been quite coincidental," Pendle said.

"Sure," I replied, "and maybe the Chinese can be trusted not to screw us on the lidanium deal, but I don't want to stake my life on it."

"Wise, I think."

"Andrea is the only member of the expedition who knows who I really am," I went on. "And, of course, my relationship with her has been accompanied by a certain amount of bloodshed."

"The incident in San Francisco might have been totally innocent," Pendle said. "The shipboard firefight might have been an assassination attempt on you which she just happened to witness. And what happened this morning might have been a rape attempt on her which *you* just happened to witness."

"You're a dreamer, Pendle."

"I was just trying to see the bright side of things. Yes, to attribute all this to coincidence strains credulity a mite. Especially since Andrea knows who you are."

I could buy the notion of the rape attempt being real. Andrea was nothing if not a spectacular-looking woman, certain to attract that sort of attention in a city like Shanghai. I could buy a Chinese thug having a Russian automatic. I could even buy the idea that Andrea showed up outside Pendle's window by coincidence. What was just too hard to swallow was the shooting on board the freighter. If that man was after me, only one person could have told him who I was—Andrea.

But who was trying to kill me? The Russians, to prevent my getting the lidanium? If they knew all about the mission, they could just wait for me to cross the border and blow me away then. They could be trying to kill me on general principles. God knows I've given them reason enough in the past. The Chinese? Maybe they figured they could get the lidanium

themselves and not have to share it with the United States. Or
they didn't trust me to obey orders and share it with them.
There were any number of possibilities.

"Maybe the attempts on my life have nothing to with
either the Chinese *or* the Russians," I said.

"Are you suggesting an outraged husband?" Pendle
laughed. "With your record, I guess its possible."

"I don't know what I'm suggesting," I replied. "I'm
going back to the ship. Andrea may still need some calming
down."

"If she doesn't," Pendle said, quite serious this time,
"Then you and I and the entire mission could be in big
trouble."

For whatever it meant, Andrea did not need calming down.
I found her on the pier, supervising the longshoremen as they
transferred the expedition's equipment from the *Rainwater* to
the *Goat*. The instant I saw her, I recognized the symptoms.
She was back in her academic shell, determined to think of
nothing but archaeology. In an attempt to bring her out of it, I
smiled and patted her on the ass.

"Stop," she said.

"My mistake," I replied, disappointed.

"Did you find out who those three men were?"

"No. There was no identification on them. That's a bit
unusual in the case of a crime which has the appearance of
being impromptu, but what the hell. Maybe they left their
wallets in the pants they sent to the dry cleaner."

"I'm glad you can joke about it," she snapped.

"The gun was Russian," I said.

If that information interested her, she didn't show it. She
kept her eyes on the Land Rover as a massive cargo boom
lowered it to the pier. Andrea was not going to have anything
further to do with me, unless it was in relation to her excavation.

Rita appeared then, all brightness and sunshine, tossing a
film cartridge into the air and catching it, over and over

again. I was grateful for the distraction.

"How was the telegraph traffic today?" I asked.

"Super. I got off a long note, and have a telephone call in for two this afternoon. What do you want to do now?"

"It doesn't matter," I shrugged, offering Rita my arm. We walked back to the city in silence.

ELEVEN

Compared with Shanghai, the port area of Tientsin where the *Goat* was moored was actually modern. Tientsin was the main Chinese port in the Gulf of Chihli, and the nearest to Peking. The capital was reachable by an eighty-mile rail link or by barge up the twisting path of the Pai-ho.

Tientsin had a newly-constructed modern port, with concrete-and-steel piers flanked by four-story, brightly-painted office buildings with large windows. The United States flag and the banners of a dozen other nations with whom the Chinese traded joined the Peoples Republic flag atop the nearest building. It was quite clearly meant to be a gesture of internationalism, a welcome. It made me uncomfortable. The damn Chinese knew all too well I was coming. Hanging out the fancy linen in honor of my arrival did nothing to buoy my spirits. And I rather liked the notion that ancient seaports should look, well, ancient. Shanghai was appropriately seedy, with an aura of danger that was amply demonstrated during my stay there. But Tientsin, at least that section of the port where the *Goat* unloaded its cargo, reminded me of a suburban American shopping mall.

The only suggestion of old technology on the pier was a single rail line, decrepit with rust, that ran halfway out to the dock. A spanking-new cargo boom worked to move the expedition's gear from the coastal schooner to a top-loading boxcar. Our stuff would travel the next leg of its journey by rail. The track followed the coast northward from Tientsin, through the eastern terminus of the Great Wall at Linyu, and up to the large cargo siding at Fuyin. There, the equipment would be transferred to three Red Army trucks for the five hundred-mile drive into the Manchurian wilds. Rita, Andrea and I would go ahead by small plane, escorted by my Chinese contact. I was due to meet the man in Tientsin. Though it didn't thrill me, the meeting was the main event of my day.

Andrea had successfully avoided me during the two days' sail up the Chinese coast from Shanghai, but Rita had proved to be a wonderful companion. She snapped pictures continuously, was terrific at conversation and professed undying love. I was beginning to enjoy being with her. I didn't believe the bit about undying love, nor did she intend it to be meant that way; but after everything I had been through it was a pleasant thing to hear.

Rita had to go to the Tientsin American Trade Mission to send more film home to New York. This mission was simple enough to find. It was the brightest of the new office buildings lining that section of the harbor, deliberately put there to welcome the expected hoards of tourists from the States. She didn't need an escort as was the case in Shanghai. I sent her off on her own and ambled in the other direction, meaning to keep a one o'clock appointment with my Chinese contact.

The geniuses at the Overseas Responsibility Group worked out with Chinese Military Intelligence a trite little ritual which I'm sure kept them amused with their own ingenuity during those long Washington lunches. I was to meet my contact in a popular tourist spot and endure one of those rituals that never happen in real-life intelligence operations.

I walked up the Pai, along the new concrete foot path, past curio shops and quayside restaurants. Across the path from them were moored a dozen native vessels, mostly sampans and small junks, with sails as brightly-colored as the banners atop the new buildings. It occurred to me that someone in the Red Chinese planning commission had visited Fisherman's Wharf in San Francisco and was attempting the same in Tientsin. There was even an open-air restaurant with barrels of steaming crabs and buckets of clams, oysters and mussels. A group of tourists, all Japanese, stood by it, taking turns having their pictures snapped.

Six blocks along the quay I found the appointed spot. It was an airy, American-style restaurant with gigantic picture windows allowing views of the carefully-staged harbor scene. It was like being in the breakfast lounge of a large Holiday Inn. There were always huge windows with a view of the Interstate. In this case, the Interstate was the broad river, slow-flowing and murky like all big rivers these days, but on its near bank crowded with colorful wharves. I looked into the restaurant. Of the forty tables, ten were occupied, a few of them by Americans.

The Americans dining that day in the Hwu Dye (Butterfly) all looked like Andrea or her colleagues at the New York Museum of Prehistory; that is to say, Ivy League casual.

As instructed, I took the two-person table in the northwest corner, away from all the other patrons. I was told to wait until my partner contacted me. Regarding the prospect dimly, I ordered a Chivas Regal on the rocks, lit a Disque Blue and stared at the other Americans, all apparently academics studying the effects of thirty-odd years of communism on the world's most populous nation. Smoking Disque Blue was like smoking a quarter-inch manila line that had been soaked in creosote, but I couldn't have my regular smokes with me. They were part of the petty drama ORG cooked up over lunch in D.C.

I ordered a dozen oysters followed by trout simmered in

white wine with almond slivers. Odd as it may sound, trout is an abundant fresh-water fish in northern China and Manchuria.

Halfway through the oysters, I saw a man staring at me from a spot toward the end of the bar. He was barely out of his twenties, slender and smooth-skinned. He looked more like a desk jockey than a fighting man. If I knew the State Department boys, this would have to be my partner. I was right. He smiled and walked over, brandishing an unlit cigarette.

"Do you have light?" he asked, his smile expanding until it was almost ear-to-ear.

"Yes," I replied, holding a match to the tip of one of my own cigarettes, the monogram N.C. looking very incorrect in the Oriental's lips.

"Custom blended, isn't it?" I asked.

"Yes. You like try one?"

"Love to." For the first time, I was enthusiastic about the exchange. I ground out my Disque Blue and took one of my own cigarettes. I lit it and inhaled with deep satisfaction.

"You like?" he asked.

"Excellent."

"Keep the pack," the man said, and took a seat without having been invited.

"My name is Pao," he went on, "and I too think this stuff with cigarettes foolish. My superiors like it, though."

"It looks good on confidential reports," I assured him.

"I will call you Dr. Rainsford, as agreed," Pao said. "Has your trip been okay?"

"Fine. No problems."

Pao couldn't avoid looking surprised. "But I thought there was a shooting! On the ship!"

"I heard the sound of shots, and there was some talk about a shooting. But there was no body, and no blood."

The Chinaman seemed stunned. He would have heard the captain's report about the sound of shots having been fired, but the only way Pao could have *known* there was a shooting was if Andrea told him. Pao might have inferred a shooting from the captain's report, especially if the man who I had the gun battle with was a Chinese agent and was conspicuous in his absence when the freighter docked in Shanghai. In any event, Pao's surprise was disconcerting.

"Well, it doesn't matter," he said, regaining his composure. "You are safe."

He hadn't asked about the trouble in Shanghai, and either didn't know or was being cautious.

"When do we take off, Pao? I'd kind of like to get on with the job."

Glad to be off the subject of past troubles, he said: "As soon as the train is loaded. That will be in two hours, maybe three. The airport is not far from here. I will have a car pick you up at the ship."

I shook my head. "I have some things to do. I mean to enjoy my meal, and then I have to clear up some details with the freight forwarding agent. When the time comes, I'll take a taxi to the airport."

"As you wish. Dr. Regan will be flying with us, and Miss Brennan?"

I nodded.

"Please explain the role of Miss Brennan. She is photographer for the expedition?"

"That's it."

"But not a scientist."

"Not so far as I can tell. Don't worry about her, Pao. I can handle the girl."

He smiled sharply, pushed back his chair and stood. "I too have things to do," he said, "and will meet you at the plane. Enjoy the cigarettes."

The Tientsin office of the Propylon Trading Company was on the top floor of one of the new buildings down the waterfront from our pier. Unlike the main office in Shanghai, this one was modern, clean and thoroughly antiseptic. For this and other reasons, Arthur Pendle was distressed.

"You're not going to like this, Nick," he said.

"I already don't like it. Pao seems to know about the shooting aboard the *Rainwater*."

"Really? That *is* bad news, if true, and it matches with one of the depressing bits of information I've got stored up for you."

"Terrific."

"Your friend, Andrea? The one with the sturdy build? Have you had much to do with her lately?"

"Not a hell of a lot."

"Well, we have finally come up with an interesting piece of background on her, one which she concealed from the official record. You recall the 1960's student unrest on American campuses?"

"Painfully," I replied.

"She was in on it. She was one of a group of young undergraduates who forcefully occupied the Columbia University administration building in 1968."

"Low Memorial Library," I replied. "It had the same architect as the New York Museum of Prehistory. She seems to have an interest in his work."

"Indeed. Anyway, Ms. Regan has for some years successfully hidden the fact that she was a member of the Weathermen, the radical arm of the Students for a Democratic Society."

"Some of whose members are still in hiding," I said.

"Yes. Her name appears on several of their recently-uncovered manifests. She seems to have quit the organization in 1970, or at least has not been active since then. In fact, she seems not to have had a political opinion at all in the past ten years. That does not, however, erase her original membership and the fact that she tried to conceal it."

"How in the hell did we end up trusting a former SDS activist with my identity?" I growled.

"ORG," Pendle replied. "She came highly recommended."

"Say no more. Jesus, Pendle, Andrea could be feeding all our movements to the other side. Furthermore, we've got *two* other sides. Does anyone know whether she was a Marxist or a Maoist?"

"Neither, and the distinctions are blurred anyway. She may just have been in the student riots as a childhood whim. She was rather on the toddler side those days. To a large extent, the American student movement was a singles club."

"A way to get laid," I said.

"Amen to that," Pendle replied. "All the same, take advantage of the fact that she seems to be ignoring you. Tell her nothing. If you can, give her the impression your mission has been scrubbed. When you disappear into the woods to cross the border in search of the lidanium, make up a convincing excuse for your absence."

"Rita will do," I nodded.

"So I understand."

"You said you had more depressing information."

"Indeed I do. Not depressing so much as perplexing. It's a message from Hawk . . . a reaffirmation of your orders."

"That's all . . . nothing new?" I asked.

"Not a bloody thing," Pendle said. "You're to trust the Chinese to the utmost, cooperate with them and turn over half the lidanium to them when you're back from the Russian side of the border."

"What the hell is that all about?" I exploded. "When have I ever needed to have my orders repeated?"

"Never that I recall."

"Damn straight never. Is this ORG again?"

" 'Fraid so, old chap," Pendle said. "I imagine your reputation for independent action scares them a little."

"I have never disobeyed orders. Not without a good reason, anyway."

"There is a chance, my good friend," Pendle went on, "that someone at ORG is afraid you will find a good reason to disobey their orders."

"Meaning that a good reason exists," I said.

"Meaning that a good reason *may* exist. Let's play along for the time being. Do as you were told to do. Find the lidanium and, if need be, use this."

He handed me a palm-sized radio transmitter built into a western-style belt buckle. "It broadcasts on two frequencies—the Chinese military frequency . . ."

"In case they prove to be worthy allies and I need their help round-about the border," I said.

"Right. And it broadcasts on the AXE frequency in case all bets with our supposed allies are off."

"Who will be listening on the AXE frequency?" I asked.

"All of us, of course, mostly by satellite. *I* will be listening from Tientsin."

"What good will that do, Pendle? Are you planning to fly in and rescue me?"

"Me? Of course not. But we do have a small naval force on maneuvers in the Sea of Japan which may be of some assistance. Let's not think negatively, Nick. I'm of the opinion the whole thing will develop smashingly."

I nodded in acquiescence, shook Pendle's hand and turned toward the door. "I have to catch a plane," I said.

TWELVE

The airport was at Hsi-ti-t'ou, a small town to the northeast of Tientsin. The town was an area of bland, concrete blocks of apartments intermixed with light industrial plants. The airfield had but two runways, and there was no control tower, only a windsock which fluttered from the top of the steel radio tower. An old and decrepit hangar had doors which looked permanently closed, and a smaller frame house, long-since converted into a pilot's shed, was just a bit less ghostly.

A brand-new, red-and-white twin-engine plane stood by the shed. It was a British Beagle B.206, an eight-seat passenger transport designed for use by businessmen. The Chinese were becoming Westernized at a furious rate. The thought still didn't make me trust them. Pao stood by it, supervising the packing of luggage for Rita and Andrea, though they had not yet arrived. I went to him.

"Where are the women?" I asked.

"Their car had a flat tire. It is being fixed now. They'll be here soon."

"How'd you know their car had a flat?"

"Radio," he said, indicating the small whip antenna atop his serviceable old Mercedes.

There was no one else within earshot, the pilot of the Beagle being inside the pilot's shed having a cup of tea. I asked, "What's your cover story, Pao? I want to know how to describe you to the rest of the expedition."

"I grew up in Harbin, in Heilungkiang province, where we are going. Tell them I am your guide and interpreter."

"I don't need an interpreter."

"But Miss Brennan? Miss Regan?"

"I get your point. How long will the flight be?"

"Half a day. We will stop at Harbin to refuel. The airplane can only fly six hundred-fifty miles without taking on additional fuel. Do you fly, Dr. Rainsford?"

"No."

I lied. If he didn't know I could fly a plane, there was little point in telling him. If he did know, my falsehood didn't register on his face, as had his surprise over my denying knowledge of the shooting aboard the China-bound freighter. If he really thought I couldn't fly, he might get careless about leaving the keys to the plane lying around. Planes were often useful things to have. If by some chance Pao did know I was lying about the plane and the shooting, it would keep him on his toes. He would spend so much time worrying what I was up to, he might make a blunder. At any rate, it would make the game more interesting.

There was a patch of dust rising from the dirt road leading to the airstrip.

"They come now," Pao said.

Andrea was all business, as usual, and aggravated with the slight delay. "Is everything stowed?" she asked me.

I said that it was.

"Who's he?" she asked, indicating Pao.

I made the introductions, depicting my Chinese partner as an expert guide, interpreter and, adding something on my

own, woodsman. I thought it might impress her. Once again I
guessed wrong. She shook hands, acknowledged his bow
without cracking a smile and peered into the luggage compartment of the B.206 Beagle to make sure all her personal
luggage was there.

Typically, Rita hugged me, then swept the lens of her
Nikon around the field. "This looks like something out of
Lindbergh. You know . . . white scarf, gloves, seat-of-
the-pants and all that."

"So take pictures of it," I said, bored wit her incessant
snapping.

"I can get this anywhere. There are hundreds of fields like
it in Kansas. Even some in New York. Show me something
interesting."

"Get in the plane," I said by way of a response.

She got in the plane, towing two camera bags behind her.

The Chinese pilot, dressed in a faded green jumpsuit, came
ambling out of the shed, carrying a thermos of tea and
looking bored. He climbed into his seat and cranked up the
engines as Pao climbed into the plane with Rita.

Andrea shouted over the noise of the twin props, "Okay,
so we're going into Manchuria. I'm doing archaeology, got
it? Just archaeology. What happens to you is your business.
Keep me out of it."

"Consider it done," I replied.

Andrea frowned and got into the plane. A few minutes
later we were off the ground and roaring north-northeast into
the heart of the Chinese-Manchurian mainland.

After refueling at the provincial capital of Harbin, we followed the path of the Sungari River for a few miles, until it
turned abruptly to the east for its eventual confluence with the
Amur. Flying at about five thousand feet, the pilot traced the
general course of the Harbin-Aihui road, a slender ribbon of
concrete which traversed the grasslands to the south side of

the Lesser Khingan Range. When the road took a brief detour
to the west into the town of Pei-an, for a few score miles we
were completely alone. The broad savannah beneath was
waist-high with wild kaoliang stalks that would, within a few
months, be as tall as American corn. In the midst of one such
plain, a small White Russian encampment was little more
than a collection of log corrals and sheep pens surrounding
ramshackle, thrown-together huts.

The Harbin-Aihui road rejoined us just in time to fit
through a valley where a break occurred in the mountains. On
Pao's instructions, the pilot dropped down to five hundred
feet. The Lesser Khingans rose dramatically on both sides,
their white-capped summits snow-covered even during the
hot Manchurian summer. We banked left and flew up the
forty-mile-wide slot between the mountains and the Amur, as
yet invisible to the north. The Khingans degenerated quickly
into the series of rolling, thickly forested hills I recalled from
the satellite reconnaissance photos. Beneath us was what
looked like a ceaseless forest, unbroken except for the now
one-lane road leading into Aihui and a small stream. The
forest was the densest I had seen; thicker even than the
Ardennes. From the low altitude of five hundred feet, not so
much as a trail could be seen.

From Aihui to Hsun-k'o on the Chinese side of the Amur,
from Belogorsk to Zavitinsk on the Russian, an area of over
six thousand five hundred square miles, a square more than
eighty miles on a side, was a nearly impenetrable carpet of
trees and streams. The Amur cut through the square, a broad,
blue ribbon which I could finally see as we approached the
end of our flight.

Aihui was a small logging town on the left bank of the
Amur. Those few permanent residents who didn't harvest the
lumber resources of the Khingan, ran small trading posts
which catered to the several tribes of nomadic hunters and
reindeer herders who passed through on their annual migra-
tions. Aihui merchants paid the tribesmen for skins, antlers

and other things they found in the forest, including paleolithic flint scraping tools. As the B.206 Beagle's twin props kicked up a small dust storm on the short dirt runway, I began to wonder if it wouldn't have been better had the nomad who picked up the stone age tool just as quickly thrown it away.

The Aihui airport was, if anything, more primitive than the one at Hsi-ti-t'ou. There was no hangar, nor any other planes. A single dirt strip paralleled the Amur, which was but half a mile to the north. A wooden shed no more than twenty feet on a side served as the only shelter, and the road leading into town was a one lane dirt road gutted by axle-busting ruts. The Chinese pilot pulled the Beagle up to the shed and cut his engines. Silence fell over the plane and its occupants. We were in the remotest part of Manchuria, a stone's throw from the most desolate part of Siberia.

I popped the door and helped the others out. Andrea was tugging eagerly at the luggage compartment latch. I took over for her. It was a simple affair; a recessed handle which required but a half-turn to the left. Andrea began pulling out the luggage, with Pao helping her. I scanned the airstrip and saw the eighteen-foot, flatbed Chinese Army truck bouncing its way up the dirt road from town. The truck had steel umbrella frames and canvas sides decorated with the gold stars-on-red-backdrop flag of the Peoples Republic of China.

"Pao," I asked, "did you call a cab?"

He squinted at the truck, then smiled. "Sure. That's me. Two men. They drive us to site. Help set up camp. Is that okay?"

"It's fine," Andrea cut in, grabbing two of her bags and striding confidently toward the truck, which had now ground to a halt not far from the plane.

"Don't you even want to see the town?" I asked her.

"No. We have work to do, Dr. Rainsford."

"But the equipment won't be here for two days," I protested.

"We can prepare for its arrival," she replied, tossing her two bags into the back of the truck before its very eager-to-please driver invited her to do so.

"Are we really going straight into the wild?" I asked Pao.

"Of course not. I stop in town. *My* orders. I hate to fly. I need food and some cold milk to rest my stomach."

"What about her determination to get right on the job?"

"So what? This my country, not hers. If she want, she can walk. I guarantee she no want."

THIRTEEN

I picked idly at a take-out portion of fried rice with braised reindeer meat as the Chinese Army truck bounced slowly up the single-lane dirt road leading out from Aihui and along the bank of the Amur. The road was more like a fire lane of the sort carved through American wilderness areas; wide enough for a jeep or small truck, yet narrow enough so that the branches could scrape ceaselessly against the roof. Angered by the detour into Aihui, Andrea sat in the absolute rear of the truck, avoiding the rest of us.

Kumara was as desolate a village as one might expect to find. It was ten miles from Aihui and consisted entirely of tiny huts on the river bank near the spot where a large stream flowed into the Amur. As our truck roared through, Manchu fishermen looked up from their nets and fish-drying racks with the casual disinterest accorded a familiar occurrence. After leaving Kumara, the road swung inland, following the course of the stream Andrea described when I first met her. Very shortly, with no warning, the truck ground to a halt.

"We are here," Pao said.

"About time," Andrea replied, pushing aside the canvas flaps and hopping from the truck. I left the others and her to unload the bags, and took a fast look around. The dirt in front of the truck was undisturbed. If a vehicle had come through that locale recently, the tracks were well hidden. Similarly, the underbrush in the direction of the dig was relatively pristine. It didn't look as if lots of people had been tramping through the area, and that was a good sign.

The dig was a hundred and fifty yards downhill, right by the edge of a swift-flowing river carrying ice cold water from the heights of the Khingans down to the Amur. Access to it was a reindeer trail which crossed the dirt road and which was marked by a swatch of red paint splattered on a tree. There was no indication of recent human traffic along the trail, the ground mosses bearing the marks of hooves but not feet.

The stream had, over the millenia, cut itself a deep slot through the stratified mountain terrain. In places the cliffs rose forty feet above the raging water. Here and there, rockslides and the heavy seasonal rains wore away patches of cliff until there remained only a moderate slope, strewn with rocks and other debris. It was on one such slope that Andrea's flint tool was found. She caught up with me and, elated, dropped her bags.

"This is beautiful," she exclaimed. "The tool must have washed down along with the rest of the seasonal runoff. The paleolithic strata should be about six feet from the present surface. We can start right in checking the cliff strata to be sure."

"Whatever you say," I replied, preferring instead to think how easy it would be to reach the Amur by following the stream.

"We'll set up camp on top of the cliff," she went on, pointing at a broad patch of deer grass atop the section of cliff nearest the slope. "Have the tents set up there, would you? I want to have a look around."

I agreed, but went up to the spot to check its suitability

anyway. It was broad enough for our five tents, but there were two dangers. First, it was a forty-foot drop almost straight down, a problem in the event of saboteurs or sleep-walkers. Second, it was too open. At two miles from Soviet territory, a camp on that site would be too simple for their border reconnaissance planes to see. When Pao came up, lugging a rolled-up canvas tent, I said, "Not here."

"Of course not. Too open. This is Miss Regan's idea?"

"Yeah," I grumbled, disliking the implications.

"We make camp in woods. Cut down a number of trees, if necessary. Maybe even be lucky enough find old native campsite. Then we can cook without worrying about smoke being seen. The Russians know where all the native campsites are."

"Are there any tribes in the area now?"

"The Mukhinos should be passing through this region now."

"Who the hell are they?"

"Manchu tribe. Very old, very small. Speak own language, too. They follow the reindeer north every year this time, crossing Amur too. Russians don't care about them."

"Interesting," I said.

"They no help to us. They keep to themselves. I go find us good campsite."

Pao went off, still lugging the rolled-up tent. I walked to the edge of the cliff and looked down. Andrea was by the edge of the stream, poking around the loose rocks with a stick. To the north, the stream continued in a relatively straight line for perhaps a half a mile, before curving sharply to the left.

Out of the corner of my eye I saw a motion in the bushes across the clearing, down the cliff line away from the direction Pao took. There was no wind, so it had to be animal or human. But what? I pretended not to notice and kept staring down the stream.

It moved again, and this time I was certain I saw *something*; a form, not tall by any means, rustled a shrub. I wheeled and ran to the spot, but by the time I arrived there was nothing to be seen. Whatever had been watching me disappeared into underbrush too thick for me to give chase.

The fire was big and lit up our whole section of the forest. Only the tops of the trees slipped away into darkness. I sipped a cup of black tea, smoked the last of my cigarettes and listened to the crackling embers. Now that the dig was actually underway, there was nothing for me to do.

Though our equipment wasn't due to arrive for another thirty six hours, Andrea had already roped off a large section of the slope into a grid, using thick twine. Each grid had a number, allowing her to catalogue items found in it. She hadn't found anything yet, save for a piece of carved bone which might be of modern vintage. I helped her set up the grid, but once that was done I had no more connection with the dig. It had been explained to Rita and the others that my job was to search for other paleolithic sites in the region. That would give me a good reason to spend a lot of time in the woods, even the several days it would take me to find the lidanium and bring it back.

Rita was asleep in her tent, and Andrea still pouring over the bit of carved bone she found. Without saying anything, I slipped out of camp. A wide deer trail ran through, a migratory route which crossed the stream a half mile to the north. I walked along it, guided by the bright moonlight. I left the camp to be alone. Yet no matter how far I went into the forest, I had the distinct feeling I had company.

The trail descended a slope like the one Andrea had mapped out, crossed the stream at an especially shallow point, then ran up a corresponding slope on the far bank and disappeared back into the forest. I picked a spot on the slope, near the water, and sat in a patch of small stones that made especially loud noises when stepped upon. I stretched out, cradled my head in my hands and pretended to go to sleep.

I lay perfectly still for nearly an hour before anything happened. The crackling of twigs came first, then the noises of the stones. There were no voices; just the sound of one man breathing laboriously. I opened my eyes a crack and saw a man bending over me. Moving quickly, I grabbed his shirt front in one hand and pressed the tip of my stiletto to his neck with the other. He said something in a guttural language I hadn't heard before, then, after a second, said, "Don't hurt me," in broken Mandarin.

I forced him to sit, let him go and looked him over with a pocket flashlight. He was an old Manchu with ghostly white hair and clothes made of deerskin. His face was reddish brown, and looked rather like the old portrait of Sitting Bull. This man, I thought, was a better connection between the natives of America and those of East Asia than anything Andrea was likely to find on her grid. I put away my knife and flicked off the lamp. Before long, I could see him well enough in the moonlight.

"Who are you?" I asked in Mandarin.

"I am Mukhino."

"The whole tribe?"

"I am Setka. I have been sent to find out who you are and what you are doing here."

"I would have thought they'd send a younger man."

"I am an elder," he replied, somewhat testily. Then with a sheepish grin, added, "And only I speak Mandarin."

"Of course. And it was you who watched me on the cliff today?"

"No. It was my granddaughter, Cila. She is only ten, and small. She can run through the bushes faster than me."

"And faster than me as well," I replied.

"That was intended. I have taught her well . . . cared for her since the damned Russians took my son and his wife and charged them with stealing. It was false, of course, but what can you say to the dogs? You are American?"

"Yes, a man of science, here to study the ways of ancient man."

Setka thought a moment, then said, "I do not understand."

"The way man lived in this land, thousands and thousands

of years ago. We look at stones, and bones, and the earth
. . ."

"Ah, yes, I remember now. The flint one of my brothers
sold in Kumara. It was that stone which brought you here all
the way from America?"

I said that it was.

"I know nothing of such things," he said, waving a
gnarled old hand in the air to indicate absence of information
and, for that matter, interest.

"We are in one of your old campsites, I think. Is that a
problem?"

"No. There are many. We have not used that one in
several years. We change sites frequently, to let the forest
replenish itself. We just wanted to know who you are."

"And now you know," I said.

"And now I know," he replied, with an enigmatic smile.

FOURTEEN

"We will move along soon," Setka told me, "to the Russian side of the River, to spend what remains of the summer."

"Several months."

"In your country, perhaps. In ours, a month at the most. Winter comes quickly here. We spend it where we have always spent it, and damn the Russians."

"Are there many Russians where you will be going?" I asked.

He shook his head. "A few. An occasional patrol. They ignore us, except when they want to accuse us falsely of stealing."

"I'm sorry about your family," I said.

"They will survive, I imagine," he replied, though without conviction. Then he added "You are very fast with a knife for a man of science."

"And you're not bad at sneaking up on men with knives."

"In these forests," he shrugged, "it is good to be skilled with a knife."

I sat on the gravel next to the wizened old man. "Where are you camped now?"

"A mile downstream, on the other bank. Would you like to visit us tomorrow?"

"Yes, very much. Can I bring you anything? Provisions? What do you need?"

"Everything we need, we make or find," he said, grumbling as he got to his feet.

By the time I got back to the expedition's camp, everyone was asleep but Pao. I found him sitting cross-legged by the fire, reheating a tin cup full of tea.

"Where you go to?" he asked.

"For a walk," I replied.

"In Manchuria, in unfamiliar territory, in the middle of the night?"

"Sure. Why not? Did you think I was going to get killed by a reindeer?"

"Reindeer not only animal in forest," Pao said, pouring himself some tea and offering me the cup, which I declined.

I went back to the tree I was leaning against earlier in the evening and sat against it. I lit up a Disque Bleu.

"Is everyone asleep?" I asked.

"Yes. How far into forest did you go?"

"Down the trail a piece. I met an old Mukhino."

This information interested Pao. "At night? In forest? They keep away from outsiders."

"This particular Mukhino was assigned to find out who we are and what we are doing here."

"He spoke Mandarin?" Pao asked, surprised.

"Yeah. I sure as hell don't speak Mukhino."

"What you tell him?"

"The standard story. That we're men of science here digging up bones."

"Did he believe it?"

"He didn't seem to *dis*believe it. I doubt he knew what I was talking about. The activity on the slope should remove any doubts. Did Andrea make anything of that bone she found?''

Pao shrugged. ''I wasn't told,'' he said.

''So you're being cut off, too.''

''Cut off?''

''Ignored,'' I explained.

''It seem that way. What her problem, anyway?''

''I couldn't begin to explain.'' I ground out the cigarette and got to my feet. ''I'm going to bed. See you in the morning.''

Pao waggled his tea cup at me as I walked across the campsite and into my tent. It was a small umbrella tent, nine-by-nine feet, just big enough for two small cots or one large one. I brought a large one with me. I had a feeling it would be needed. It was.

Rita was zipped into my double sleeping bag, her bare arms and shoulders protruding. She looked up at me with sleepy eyes.

''Don't you ever sleep alone?'' I asked, sitting on the edge of the cot to pull off my boots.

''Not when you're available,'' she replied.

The temperature dropped down to a chill fifty degrees that night, but began climbing rapidly as soon as the sun was over the horizon.

I wanted to visit the Mukhino camp first thing, but had to do it alone. Rita was set on going along. She had taken all the pictures she cared to of the slope and the grid, and, with the rest of the equipment not due to arrive until the end of the day, was bored.

''I don't understand why you won't take me,'' she said, pouting.

''Not won't. *Can't.*''

''Why not? I can walk, too.''

''I'm going over some pretty rough terrain.''

''I can handle it. I want to take pictures of that tribe. A tiny group of nomads practically unknown outside of Manchuria? You can't leave me at camp.''

"I'm sorry, Rita.''

"What's this tribe got to do with your work, anyway?'' she asked, turning angry. "You're supposed to be digging up bones.''

"Wrong. I'm supposed to be scouting for possible other sites where Andrea can dig up bones. This tribe may be of some use. Do you understand?''

"I understand that I want to go along.''

I shook my head. "Absolutely not.''

"Dammit, Paul!'' she cried.

"Let's make a deal. If the trail proves easy enough, I'll take you along on another day.''

"Not good enough,'' she snapped.

"It will have to do,'' I snapped back.

Rita swept up a Nikon, slung the strap over her head and stomped off angrily in the direction of the slope where, although it was just a little after dawn, Andrea was already at work.

I tied on my hiking boots and stood. I had my old clothes for the occassion—faded jeans, an old Army jacket, and a red-and-white plaid flannel hunting shirt. The belt Pendle gave me, with its tricky buckle, was strapped around the pants. I wanted to look like a slightly seedy professor of archaeology who might seem at home tramping around the Manchurian wilds. For added effect, I took Rita's small Yashica.

After taking the trouble to make sure no one followed me, I took the reindeer trail north along the west bank of the stream until I reached the second slope where, the night before, I met Setka.

The slope was deserted, but the stream at that point was only fifty feet wide and easily fordable. I jumped along a series of flat rocks clearly placed there by the Mukhinos for such purposes, and was soon on the other shore. There, the deer trail continued inland, but an ancillary, much narrower trail followed the course of the right bank of the stream. It was this smaller trail that I took. I wasn't sure why; the way was difficult, leading sharply uphill and running in many places along the exact edge of the forty-foot precipice. But taking the broad trail straight into the Mukhino camp struck me as being too obvious. And I wanted to see what was to be found in the little-seen parts of the valley. You never knew when it might be useful to have a secret place in which to hide.

The narrow trail was bare of vegetation—not because of frequent use, but because the ground was rocky and sandy, and swept by frequent rain floods. Walking along it was tricky business; I had to keep my right hand on the vegetation to the land side of the precipice to keep my balance. Even so, every other stop sent pebbles flying out into the abyss.

The cliff rose even higher, now sixty feet above the riverbed, and the drop was still straight down! Through the brush to the front of me I looked up the hill and saw the hint of a clearing, a spot where the trail broadened into a ledge, perhaps thirty feet across, between the precipice and another, higher extension of the mountain rising far above it. There was something else; motion, like I had seen the day before, closer to the camp.

I had been walking in almost complete silence. I stopped entirely and dropped into a crouch, watching the clearing through five feet of underbrush. A young girl, barely ten years of age, stood looking in my direction, wondering if she had heard something. After half a minute, she seemed to have decided she had not. She went back to what she was doing— building twigs and small sticks into the proper, conical shape for a Mukhino fire. She was short and slight, with the same dark skin and features as the old tribesman I had met the night before, and was dressed in the same deerskins. Cila, I thought, Setka's granddaughter. Smiling at having sneaked up on *her* for a change, I stood and took a step through the brush toward her.

It was a mistake. I startled the child, and she lurched

backwards toward the precipice. The pebbles gave way beneath her feet as they had beneath mine. She screamed as her feet went out from under her and she slid, feet first, over the edge.

I crashed through the bushes and made a diving leap, skidding across the ground on my belly and clutching her wrist.

She dangled, yelling in the Manchu tongue I couldn't possibly understand, her legs kicking wildly six stories above the rocky stream bed. I tightened my grip and flexed my bicep, pulling her up to safety in one smooth stroke.

She lay on the cliff bank for a moment, whimpering and shaking, now and then looking at me with the wild eyes of fear.

"Cila," I said, hoping the sound of her voice would calm her.

It didn't. She scrambled to her feet and ran off, losing herself in the underbrush to the north. I knew chasing her would be futile, and didn't try.

I got to my feet, sighed and brushed myself off. I tore a pants leg when I skidded across the clearing. Fixing it would give Rita something to do, I thought.

The clearing was one of the highest points in the area, and a natural fortification. The cliff which rose some twenty feet above it was unscalable. A man with a gun, or, for that matter, a flint axe, could almost hold off an army. It looked as if someone had indeed done so, because to the inland side of the clearing was a small cave cut into the cliff wall. The entrance to it was partially covered with hanging vines and small sticks, the latter recently put up.

The little Mukhino girl was using the clearing and the cave as her personal play place. Probably, no one else knew about it. I pushed aside the sticks and stepped inside, lighting the way with a pocket flashlight.

The cave was deep and dry. The ceiling was low, for the ground had been built up by years upon years of long-ago

habitation. Toward the entrance, I could see the results of
Cila's playing; the floor was swept clean and a bundle of
kindling arranged neatly by one wall. But deeper into the
cave, where the little girl had not dared go, I found myself
stepping into history. The floor was littered with pieces of
flint, bones of both humans and animals, some of them
charred by fire. On the walls, the outlines of mastiffs, cave
bears and long-extinct species of caribou were drawn in
yellow and red. Even though I was only playing at being an
archaeologist, I knew exactly what I had found. Leaving it
undisturbed, I decided to return to camp to tell Andrea.

FIFTEEN

"This is incredible," Andrea said, "absolutely incredible."

"I had a feeling you'd like it," I replied, quite justifiably proud of myself.

"You've earned your pay for the week, Dr. Rainsford. I forgive you for everything that's happened."

"I'm off the hook, huh?"

"Completely. I still don't want anything to do with your *other* reason for being here, but as an archaeologist you've earned your place in history. This find will have your name on it, of course."

"Out of the question," I said, standing and nearly banging my head on the ceiling. Andrea had rigged up a portable lamp, but the inside of the cave remained dark and foreboding.

"That's the way things work with scientific discoveries," she insisted.

"Not this one. You found it, not me. You were hiking in

the woods and there it was. My cover as Dr. Rainsford won't hold up if I start making discoveries.''

"That's not fair," Andrea said.

"Life is tough all around."

"But I accept anyway. The discovery will look better on my resumé than on yours. Thanks, Paul.''

"You're welcome.''

"And now, if you'll excuse me, there must be six feet of datable strata in here." She poked a finger gently down into the top layer of soft dirt, and almost immediately felt a bone. She smiled, and I felt good about it. At the very least, it would keep her out of my hair while I completed my mission. And I was getting tired of apologizing to her for saving her life.

Bending low, I walked back out into the daylight. Already, the clearing was filling up with people. The expedition's equipment had arrived, and with it Andrea's two assistants from the museum. Rita was there, snapping away at the stream far below us. Sitting on a rock by the entrance to the trail, Pao looked vaguely amused.

"So, we have real discovery," he said.

"It looks that way."

"Peking will be twice happy. The American archaeologist assigned to look for ancillary sites actually found one. I think it funny."

"So do I, my friend, but I have better things to do than laugh. I have to find the Mukhinos."

"Do not bother. Mukhinos find you. Look.''

He pointed across the clearing to the trail leading north. Cila was there, standing demurely at the edge of the clearing, looking at me. I smiled and went to her. Without saying a word, she took my hand and led me down the trail.

Unlike the southern trail, the northern route was relatively easy, being both downhill and further from the precipice. The little girl led me a half mile away from the clearing to a point where the trail split in two, the left-hand fork descending into a glade where short pines and patches of deer grass were combined like a chess board. It was the Mukhino camp, and Setka, the old man, saw me immediately.

He rushed the length of the camp, surprisingly agile for a man his age, as a group of curious men and women gathered in his footsteps.

Setka hugged me, tears streaming down his reddish-brown cheeks. "You saved my granddaughter. She is all that's left of my family, and would have died. You saved her."

"I also frightened her into falling," I replied.

"No. She is a young girl, and young girls frighten easily. She should not have been on the cliff. When she told me what happened, I made her go back and bring you here. You can have any favor you ask. You are a hero."

"I'm no hero," I laughed, "but I'll have a cup of tea. And I wouldn't mind some advice."

"Anything," he said, and brought me across the camp to his fire, the little girl and some of the curious following.

The Mukhino camp was much as I had imagined it—small, round huts made of sticks covered with deerskin, each with its own fire and, hanging from nearby tree limbs, newly killed rabbits, deer and fowl. Like everyone in that land, Setka had a pot of coarse black tea brewing at all times, and poured some into a tin cup of a sort I had seen in the shops at Kumara.

The entire camp must have heard of my having saved Cila, for it wasn't too long before several dozen men, women and children were standing or sitting near Setka's fire, listening in rapt silence to a conversation in a language none of them understood.

I took the latest satellite reconnaissance map of the region and spread it on the ground before him, then pressed a fingertip against the circle of fire ten miles inside the Russian border which marked the impact point of the deep space asteroid.

"Do you know this place?" I asked.

The old man peered at the map, using his own fingertip to trace the lines of familiar streams, ridges and roads.

"Of course. It is our summer hunting ground. It is the farthest north we go. We leave for that place tomorrow. There is a spot where the Amur can be forded when the water is low. There."

He pointed at the juncture of the stream and the Amur. Apparently, the stream cut a sand bar into the upstream side of its confluence with the larger waterway. It was useful information.

"What is this round spot on the map?" he asked.

"Fire," I said, "caused by a meteorite."

"I do not understand."

"A falling star."

The old man thought for a moment, then nodded. "I have heard of such things. In Tunguska, when I was a boy, one of these falling stars caused much damage."

"Much more than this one. But I want to see it anyway."

"You will go into Russia?" he asked, astonished.

"Yes."

"With us?"

"No, not with you. That might get you in trouble with the Russians. I will go the day after, and secretly."

"I am not afraid of the Russian dogs," he spat.

"No, but I am. This must be done my way. Are there patrols in the area?"

"No, never. It is much too thick a forest. There are no roads, only deer trails. I can draw them on the map, if you have a pencil."

I did, and he traced the route the tribe would take the following day, consulting with several younger men, who nodded their approval and babbled in Mukhino.

When I thanked him, Setka returned the pencil and said, in a low voice, as if there were anyone else about who could understand Chinese, "Then you are more than a man of science, as I suspected."

I nodded. "But no one must know, especially not the Russians."

"No one will know," Setka replied with a tone of absolute certainty.

There was a stirring of excitement in the crowd, and I looked up to see Rita walking toward me from the far side of the camp. I swore to myself, quickly rolled up the map and hid it inside my jacket.

"Who is this woman?" Setka asked.

"A friend," I said reluctantly. "She wants to take photographs of your camp. Is that all right?"

"Of course," he laughed. "You are both at home here."

I went to her, took her by the shoulders and asked angrily, "What the hell are you doing here?"

"I followed you and the little girl."

"I know *how* you got here. What I want to know is *why*."

"To take pictures, of course. What did you think?"

"I think you're going to get yourself killed running around the woods by yourself. This isn't Central Park, you know."

"I'm safer here than in Central Park. Come on, Paul, this place is fabulous. Let me shoot a couple of rolls. I'll be in and out in ten minutes."

She would do what she wanted anyway. "Don't give them any trouble," I said, as she scurried off to point her camera at the patient and somewhat amused natives.

While she was busy, I said goodbye to the old man, never expecting to see him again. I would be in and out of the meteorite impact site faster than Rita would buzz through the Mukhino camp. And I planned to stay away from the tribe while there, just to avoid bringing them trouble.

"I told her to behave herself," I said.

"She will cause no trouble, I am sure. In any case, I owe you everything. Come. I will tell you the history of my tribe, and you can tell her. She will have nice photographs when she goes home to America."

SIXTEEN

I lost a day without even thinking about it. Andrea and the rest of the expedition were busy transferring equipment from the old camp to a new one hacked out of the forest near the cave. Rita was kept occupied taking pictures of the transfer. Pao and I went over the map the Mukhinos had modified for me. I didn't tell him the pencil outlines of deer trails and migratory routes came from their information. In case my Chinese partners were planning a double-cross, I didn't want the Mukhinos to get in trouble.

The night before Pao and I were to leave for the border figured to be a problem. Rita had been all over me the whole time I was in Manchuria. But when I told her Pao and I were going off on a three-day exploration hike in search of more sites, Rita merely shrugged. "I'm getting sick of Manchuria anyway," she said, and went off to sleep in her own tent for the first time.

I had a night alone at last, and fell asleep listening to the hooting of a nearby owl and the soft crackling of the fire outside my tent. The alarm awoke me an hour before dawn, and by the time Pao poked his head inside the tent, I was ready to go.

"Where your girl?" he asked.

"Bored. It was bound to happen."

"This pretty boring part of China for a city girl," Pao replied.

How did he know she was a city girl? I never mentioned she was a New Yorker, but I suppose she might have.

"You ready?" he asked.

"Yeah. Are you armed, Pao?" I showed him my shoulder holster, with the handgrip of Wilhelmina poking angrily from it.

He replied by opening his drab green jacket and patting the butt of a spanking-new Chinese silenced pistol, that curious amalgam of single-shot and semiautomatic handgun.

"Do you like that thing, Pao?"

"Sure."

"I find it pretty noisy on semiautomatic operation."

"We Chinese only need one shot," he said with a toothy grin.

"Sure," I replied, buttoning my jacket and straightening it. "It occurs to me that while you know a lot about me, I know almost nothing about you."

"I'm only in field a few years," Pao replied. "You one famous man."

I made no reply, and he added, "They pick me because I know this territory."

"So you said. Well, let's go."

"I make sure nobody looking."

He poked his head outside my tent and took twenty seconds to scan the other tents in the compound.

"Nobody looking," he replied.

"I'll rely on your judgment," I said dryly, taking a quick look myself before leading the way out of the umbrella tent and into the cool Manchurian dawn.

There was a low fog in the predawn hours, and the first rays of sunlight fell on a forest ground heavy with dew. We skirted the cave, which had a twenty-four-hour guard, and picked up the deer trail later on, following it into the old Mukhino camp. Abandoned but a day, the clearing scarcely showed signs of human habitation: a few scarred patches of soil where the fires had burned, and the circular holes of rough-cut hut supports. The tribe was in the habit of leaving its camp grounds in much the same condition it found them.

I carried a standard canvas hiking pack; nothing fancy, as long as you ignored the two-man inflatible boat, its CO_2 cartridge, the compact Geiger counter adjusted to read lidanium, the lead-lined fabric pouch to carry the heavy element in and the assortment of stainless-steel digging tools. The pack weighed in at more than forty pounds, and I would have to haul that amount better than twelve miles.

We didn't follow in the tracks of the Mukhinos, but took a shorter route which was too narrow for the tribe, its animals and equipment. The trail led north, following the general contours of the stream. The way was all downhill, leading to the Amur just as that massive river went into a sharp turn to the southeast. The Amur was a quarter mile wide at that point and flowed with a current of about four knots. Most of its length, the Amur was twice as wide with half the current, and navigable at all but low water all the way from Nikolayevsk on the Tatar Strait to the Mongolian border. But where we stood, the Amur was fast and shallow, the lack of depth owing mainly to input from the stream.

I set down my pack and laboriously pulled out the inflatable boat.

"We can ford the river," Pao said.

"Not now we can't. The water's high. Look at the bank. Besides, I'd rather use the boat. It will be faster on the way back. We may need to be paddling like hell."

He nodded grimly and checked his watch. "The Russian patrol is due any minute," he said.

"What's their schedule?"

"They fly down the river from Blagoveshchensk to Trygda every two hours. A small plane, flying at about five hundred feet. It is due at this location at approximately a quarter after the hour."

"What's the reason for this patrol? Supposedly the only ones crossing the river here are the Mukhinos, who the Russians don't care about."

"We understand it's to keep an eye on navigation," Pao replied with a shrug. "It may be true. I have heard the flights are mainly to carry mail and provisions from one outpost to another. I think half the time they don't bother to look down."

"Don't count on it, pal. I'm not going to blow up this boat until that plane is long gone. Come on, let's get out of sight."

I moved Pao behind a small stand of sugar pines, the lower branches of which effectively shielded us from view from above.

"Do they run patrol boats?" I asked.

"No. Navigability is too unpredictable. They run supply barges, but only once a week. The next one isn't due until Thursday. We will be quite safe from notice by water."

"Uh huh," I replied.

Right on schedule, a twin engine Beriev which bore the markings of the Red Army soared overhead, following the course of the Amur. The second it was gone, I moved back into the open, screwed the CO_2 cannister onto the valve of the raft and watched it inflate. It was eight feet long, and painted green and brown camoflage for the time it would be hidden in the bushes on the far side of the Amur.

I withdrew two collapsing aluminum oars from my pack and shoved the raft into the water.

"Come on," I said, stepping into it and taking a seat, "Mother Russia beckons."

Pao smiled, but without much sincerity, and joined me in sitting cross-legged in the tiny rubber boat.

"I hope you're enjoying this as much as I am," I said, and pushed away from shore.

The crossing of the Amur was uneventful, as I had hoped.

The current carried us a mile downstream and around the bend in the fifteen minutes it took to paddle over to the Russian side. This was planned for in the maps I drew up, and we landed in a small, marshy cove where a tiny, seasonal rivulet added its small amount of water to the Amur. We pulled the raft onto the bank and cut enough underbrush to cover it up from all but the closest search.

There had been no river traffic during the crossing and no further planes. The area looked as devoid of human life as its reputation made it out to be. That was fine with me. I checked the map, confirming that Pao and I would have to trek a mile up the rivulet before picking up the first passable trail. At least, walking ankle-deep in water, we were unlikely to run into Russian patrols.

The rivulet was never more than ankle-deep, and there were still no signs of human life. This was all to the good. At the appointed spot, the rivulet twisted to the left and Pao and I stepped ashore onto a narrow trail that recently had been trampled by hundreds of hooves.

"Safe enough for you, eh?" Pao asked.

I nodded, but without true feeling. I would feel safe when I was back in the USA, having one of my cigarettes and drinking a glass of Chivas, unafraid of telling the world who I was.

"We still have eight miles to go," I said. "Let's not get to feeling that this job is going to be easy."

"You Americans," he laughed. "You always expect the worst."

"Sure we do. That way it hurts less when the worst happens." I started on up the narrow deer trail. "Come on, Pao. Let's get this job over with. I have a bad feeling about all this peace and quiet."

He smiled and followed. I sensed he was humoring me. This was, to him, a lark; a first assignment for a young agent, something carried out on his home turf. He seemed to think of it as being akin to poaching trout on a private game preserve. If you were caught, you were spanked and thrown the hell out.

I was right, of course. Two miles further on, the narrow trail crossed a wide one. This wide trail had not been described to me as such by Setka. He said it was one of the many small, insignificant side trails with which I should not concern myself.

Pao was alarmed, and he reached for his weapon. I knelt by the side of the larger trail. It was six feet wide, worn down to the sand by narrow tire tracks, the bushes along both sides crudely hacked away in spots.

"Russians not supposed be patrolling here," Pao said.

"Well, somebody sure the hell is, and if it ain't the Russians, I don't know who."

"But my information . . ."

I cut him off with a wave of the hand. Coming from the east, from the direction of the border outpost at Trygda, was the beating of a single cylinder.

"Motorcycle patrol," I said, diving into the bushes.

SEVENTEEN

Pao's reflexes weren't as good as mine. Before he could throw himself into the undergrowth, the cycle was around a bend and upon him. He wisely dropped his hands to his sides and stood in the middle of the trail, looking embarrassed but no doubt feeling terrified.

The cycle looked nearly of World War II vintage. It was a battered brown 750cc, with a sidecar that had been decorated a long time ago with a red star. The man riding in the sidecar carried a 7.62mm RPD light machine gun and looked as if he were scarcely out of his teens. I slipped my Beretta into my palm and waited.

The cycle ground to a halt just beyond my hiding place and the man in the sidecar jumped out. He stuck the muzzle of his RPD in Pao's gut and asked in Mandarin, "Who are you?"

Pao kept his cool. "A hiker," he said. "Lost. I do not know this territory. Who are *you*?"

The Russian soldiers exchanged quizzical looks. The one with the machine gun said, "Soviet Army patrol from

Trygda. You are on our side of the border. Are you saying you don't know?''

Pao shrugged. "I saw no border. No signs.''

"The Amur is the border,'' the Russian said, angrily this time. "Certainly you saw the Amur.''

"I waded across a river. Is that the Amur?''

"You will have to come with us.''

"I am from south, from Peking. A technician with a scientific expedition in Manchuria. I went for hike, got lost. That is all.''

"You will come with us,'' the man said, giving Pao a vicious poke with the muzzle of his rifle.

I never could figure out if at that instant Pao lost his cool or took his opportunity. I don't suppose it mattered. Pao swept the point of the rifle aside with one hand. The Russian's finger closed on the trigger, and a spray of 7.62mm slugs tore uselessly into the underbrush. At the same time, Pao drove the knuckles of his right fist into the Russian's solar plexus. The man went all white and doubled over, in time to meet Pao's knee coming up. He fell to the ground, gasping and spouting teeth and blood.

The driver of the cycle was astonished for a second, and hesitated. Then he reached for a belt holster. I stood, aimed the Beretta at his head and shouted "freeze" in Russian.

He froze. Pao went quickly to him and relieved him of his weapon.

I came out of the bushes, pulled the soldier off his cycle and backed him up against the trunk of an old pine.

"Talk," I said.

"What do you want to know?'' he asked, clearly terrified.

"How long have you been patrolling this route?''

"A . . . a month . . . no more.''

"This route starts at Trygda? Where does it end?''

"Blagoveshchensk.''

"All that way by cycle? Why?''

"It was judged that the territory was improperly patrolled.''

"That's all?"

"That's all I was told."

I pressed the muzzle of my automatic against the man's cheek and said, "I hope you're telling the truth."

"I'm not afraid to die," he said, with bravado that struck me as being entirely false.

"Who said anything about dying? I was going to shoot your balls off. One at a time."

I lowered the gun to his crotch. He got the message, and the bravado disappeared.

"I—I—" he stammered.

I holstered the gun, and showed the man my satellite recon map of the area. I pointed out the asteroid impact spot.

"What do you know of this?" I asked.

"Uhh . . . nothing . . . what is it?"

"A burned-out area six miles north of here. What do you know of it?"

"Uhh . . . nothing. I swear it. There are no patrols up there. Just here, closer to the river."

"If you're lying to me, son, you're gonna be singing soprano tomorrow."

"I tell the truth," he said.

"Tell me about your patrol. Do you report in by radio?"

"No. We have no radio."

"How long before you're due in Blagoveshchensk?"

"Four hours. It is a long trip."

"And how long after that before they send someone out to look for you?"

"I'm not sure," he said. "We broke a chain once, and sat six hours before help came. There is only one patrol a day."

I stepped away from the man and sighed. Pao was holding the Russian machine gun at the ready. I knew what he was thinking, and shook my head.

"There's no point in killing them. The Russians will be after us in ten hours anyway. We have their cycle now. We can find the goods and be gone in half that time. Let's tie them up and leave them in the woods."

I spoke in Mandarin, which the Russian cycle driver must have not understood. He took my reprieve as being a death sentence, and promptly turned it into one. He screamed "no" and bolted down the trail. Pao wheeled and, acting instinctively, blew him all to hell with the Soviet RPD. A half-dozen slugs tore open the man's chest, lifted him entirely off the ground and dropped him like a satchel of wet rags in the middle of the newly-widened trail.

"Damn," I said, under my breath so as not to make Pao feel worse.

"He ran," Pao exclaimed. "I had to shoot him."

"Of course you did. Come on, let's tie up the other one. He sure as hell isn't going anywhere, and he didn't overhear the talk about the impact zone so he can't lead his pals there."

Pao hesitated, perhaps feeling regret, although both of us knew we were better off with one of the Russians dead. I took the RPD from Pao and squeezed his arm. "You're a lot handier to have around than I'll admit I thought you were going to be," I said. "The way you handled yourself when that cycle ran up to you was pretty impressive. I'll tell you what, Pao. If the both of us survive this ordeal, I'll give you a recommendation you can have engraved in bronze and hung on the Great Wall."

It took us half an hour to clean up the mess. I carried the driver's body a hundred feet into the woods and covered it with leaves, pine needles and dried sticks. The wounded man was tied up hand and foot, gagged, and tressed to a sapling pine a hundred yards into the forest. Spilled blood was covered over with sand along the trail, and Pao and I carried the Russian motorcycle an eighth of a mile up our original path to obscure the direction we had taken. Then we hopped aboard, with me driving and Pao riding shotgun, and headed north toward the impact zone.

The Russian motorcycle changed the entire course of events. Instead of a two-day hike from our camp in Manchuria to the impact zone in Russia, we found ourselves at the rim of the designated territory by mid-afternoon of the first day. The sight was amazing: a mile from ground zero the landscape altered drastically. Although it was the height of the growing season, all the leaves were gone from the trees as if sucked off by a gigantic vacuum cleaner. Three-quarters of a mile from ground zero, the bark on the north side of all the trees was charred. Half a mile from where the meteorite impacted, only the strongest trees remained upright, charred and lifeless hulks, and all the underbrush was burned away. But it was when we reached the perimeter of the area that the sight was really memorable.

An entire, quarter-mile circle had simply been blasted from the face of the earth. Nothing was left standing, and the charred remains of trees of all sizes lay flat, their roots pointed toward the center of the circle. I tried to imagine the moment of impact; a sudden brightening of the sky, a shock wave and a flash of fire, then the shattering impact when, for a microsecond, a little bit of the sun was created here in the Siberian wilds.

A line of people, single file and looking as forlorn as a Bedouin caravan, wound across the zone of devastation toward me. I shut down the motorcycle engine and stepped off the machine, as Pao climbed out of the sidecar.

It was the Mukhinos, on the move again, this time heading back south. Leading the trek was the old man, who embraced me and, with tears in his eyes, said, "It is the cauldron of hell. Everything is dead . . . the trees, the animals, the entire forest. The herds are shunning this entire region. We are going back across the river."

"I'm sorry," I said.

"I am sorrier for you. *This* is what you travelled halfway around the world to see?"

"This is it."

He shook his head sadly.

"If it's any consolation," I went on, "I don't plan to stay long. We borrowed this machine, and its original owners aren't too happy about the idea.''

Setka scowled at the red star emblazoned on the side of the cycle.

''This land is ruined for us. First the Russians, now this. We must go. Be careful, my young friend.''

''And you too, old man,'' I replied, shaking Setka's hand for what I was certain would be the last time.

EIGHTEEN

With the Mukhinos gone, I said "Come on, let's find the lidanium and get the hell out of here."

"What big hurry?" Pao asked. "We only steal cycle an hour ago. They not know about it for half a day yet."

"And that patrol those two guys were on wasn't supposed to exist. I don't like loose ends, especially when I'm ten miles deep into Russian territory. Turn the cycle around and aim it back down the trail."

As he did what he was told, I took off my pack and from it withdrew the Geiger counter that AXE had disguised as a pocket calculator and tuned to the frequency of radioactive lidanium.

I switched on the device. When the square root button was depressed, there appeared in the center of the LED readout a zero which moved to the right or left depending upon the relative location of the lidanium. I tried it out, scanning the burned-out area, and all the while the zero kept aimed in the direction of the center of the circle.

"You find it?" Pao asked.

"Yeah, I found it. Stay here and keep that cycle ready to take off. I hear tell that lidanium doesn't come in large enough amounts to prevent me digging it up by myself."

Pao nodded, and I got my metal shovel and walked to the center of the circle. It wasn't rough going. Up that close, the trees were little more than ashes, and crumbled beneath the soles of my boots, sending puffs of ash into the mid-day sky. As I neared the impact point, the silence of the place became overwhelming. After spending several days during which I was never without a cover of leaves over my head, being out in such a desolate, empty space was strange.

The epicenter was as I expected. The deep space meteorite, composed mostly of lighter elements, had not carved a deep hole in the ground but had exploded on impact, building a small cone not unlike those in the centers of lunar craters. Rays of cosmic material shot out from the base of the cone a distance of twenty or thirty feet before becoming indistinguishable from the black charcoal and gray ash of the fire. The cone was five feet high. I circled it, trying the counter in various positions, until I could guess that the lidanium was embedded about two feet below normal ground level, beneath the center of the cone. Being heavier than the rest of the asteroid, the lidanium would be buried the deepest. I put aside the Geiger counter and started digging.

The cosmic material was light and crumbly, like moon rock and, once the crust of the cone was shovelled away, uniformly dark gray. I worked as fast as I could, and the cone soon was leveled, leaving only a shallow depression in the earth. In the middle of that pan-shaped depression was a fist-sized hole. The midday sun shone straight down the hole and glinted off a large chunk of the metal I had come so far to get.

I fumbled through my pack for the metal-lined carrying pouch and the tongs. I didn't really need the tongs since lidanium was only dangerous with prolonged exposure. If I juggled that silver-gray chunk for two hundred hours or more, I might be in danger of having my chromosomes rearranged. That failing, the lead pouch would be entirely safe. All I had to do was beat it back across the border, divide the spoils with the Chinese and go home. Or so said the orders from Washington.

Using the tongs, I pulled the chunk from the hole; then, taking the scientists' word for my safety, I picked the chunk of metal up in my hand. It was heavy but soft; my fingernail made a clear line on its surface. I put it in the pouch, tossed away the tongs and started back to where Pao was waiting.

"Find it?" he asked.

"Yeah. Let's get the hell out of here."

"I'll drive. I'm good at this. You ride shotgun."

I shrugged, but asked "Where'd you pick up that expression, Pao? 'Ride shotgun'?"

"John Wayne movie, where else? Here, you take Russian gun."

I smiled and got into the sidecar. Pao had certainly proved himself in combat, and he no doubt could drive a cycle as well. "We'll go a mile to the south, then take that wider trail which splits off to the west. You remember the one?"

"Sure."

I rested the Soviet RPD across my lap, leaned back and closed my eyes for what I hoped would be a smooth and, most importantly, fast trip back to the border. "Try not to hit any bumps, Pao. I feel I've earned my wages for today."

He kicked over the engine and the motorcycle started back down the trail toward China. It was all so easy. With a little more luck, I thought, we might just pull this job off. I should have known better.

When we rounded a turn and headed toward the intersection with the wide trail we found it blocked by two Russian cycles.

Pao screeched to a halt. "Damn," he said in faultless English.

"No kidding. Ram it straight down their throats, Pao. Wind this thing up as hard as you can, I'll keep their heads down and we'll bail out at the last minute. I'll dive left and you go right. We'll take it from there."

He nodded grimly and pushed the accelerator as far forward as it would go. At the same time, I leveled the RPD at the Russian trail-block and opened fire. They must have been expecting surrender or an attempt to reverse course and run. Our frontal assault caught the four men manning the blockade entirely off guard. They dived behind their machines as my slugs tore all around them.

The acceleration toward the blockade took less than ten seconds. Pao and I bailed out, jumping left and right, a second before impact. The two Russian cycles opposing us were lined up one in front of the other. Our cycle hit the first of theirs and blew up, the gas tanks exploding simultaneously. The flash lit up the forest, and the roar must have deafened the blockade's defenders. I rolled through a patch of thorns, and came up firing.

In finishing up the RPD's magazine I tore all hell out of the second cycle and saw one Russian soldier stick his head above the bushes and have it just as quickly removed. There was a brief scream, then nothing but the sound of burning gasoline. That left three.

I had no idea where Pao ended up, but I heard firing that hit nowhere near me and seized the opportunity to move. I took three steps and dived through more thorns, rolling again and coming to a crouch behind a fat old tree. I pulled out my automatic, took a deep breath and, with the gun in front of me, swung around the tree.

A young Russian soldier was no more than twenty feet from me, approaching the tree in a near crouch but aiming his RPD at the wrong side of the trunk. Startled, he swung the muzzle toward me, too late. I fired one shot which caught the man in the chest, spun him around and dropped him.

A burst of slugs tore into my tree and I ducked back behind

it. There was a long period of silence, some approaching footsteps, then a single shot. I wheeled around the tree, the other side this time, to see Pao waving at me from behind the burning hulk of our motorcycle.

"Got him!" he shouted. "You okay?"

"Get down!" I yelled. "This isn't a carnival."

My warning was too late. There was a burst of shots and Pao was hurled to the ground.

The shots came from behind him. I hit the deck and crawled on my belly toward my fallen companion. The body of the Russian Pao had shot lay twitching in the briars. I relieved him of his machine gun and continued on. Pao was lying beside our cycle, sweating in torrents, a trickle of blood seeping from the corner of his mouth.

"Sorry," he whispered, and died.

"I'll have the bastard's ass, Pao," I whispered back, and crawled past him to a point where I could see behind the jumble of the three cycles. The fourth Russian lay on the ground, on his side, bleeding from an abdominal wound. His RPD lay limply by an outstretched hand. He was alive, but the recoil of having shot Pao was too much. The gun was out of his grasp and he hadn't the strength to get it back. He stared at me with wild eyes as I crawled up to him and pressed the muzzle of my RPD against his cheekbone.

"No," he gasped.

"You were waiting for us. How did you know we were here?"

"Our patrol."

"Bullshit. They had no radio and you had no time to find them. And the one who lived didn't know where we were going. Who told you?"

He shook his head, the motion bringing him pain, and said again, "No."

I growled and pulled back on the trigger, holding it down until all that was left of the man's head was a red and gray sodden mass which resembled jelly more than anything else.

I lay still a moment, watching blood spurt from the severed arteries in the man's neck, until I was sure he was the last of them on the scene.

I got to my feet. There were no other living souls in sight, only blood and burned-out woodland. But the third Russian cycle seemed in pretty good shape. Only the sidecar was damaged by fire, and that I was able to detach by simply twisting the locking bars. I turned it around and fired it up, after reloading the RPD with a fresh clip.

I couldn't take the trail I had planned. If a bunch of Russians were waiting for me on this one, they'd be waiting on the other. I had to pick a route totally off-the-wall. Checking my map, I found the most obscure trail Setka had marked out for me. It swung five miles out of the way, and dangerously close to the Russian base at Trygda. But I felt sure nobody would think of looking for me there. With the machine gun slung over my neck and hanging in front of me ready for use, I aimed the front wheel in that direction and roared off.

A mile down the road I had another idea and stopped. I opened my pack and took out the lidanium. I took off its lead-lined wrapper, tossed the pouch far into the woods, then kicked the rare element around on the ground until it acquired a superficial coating of dark loam. It looked black as coal, although it was a hell of a lot heavier. In my bag I had a replacement pair of woolen socks. I slipped one inside the other and dropped the lidanium into it, knotting the open end of the sock. Suddenly I had another weapon, or at least a crudely-improvised cosh which actually was created to conceal the true value of its weight. I stuck the whole thing back in my pack and continued on. The protective lead was gone. If the Russians caught me, which was getting to be a distinct possibility, the least thing I would have to worry about was chromosome damage.

I knew that sooner or later I would have to cross the trail the Russians widened to facilitate their new Trygda-

Blagoveshchensk patrol. It seemed likely for them to be on that trail in force, guarding all the crossings. They had quite definitely been tipped off, but not all that far in advance of my entry into Russian territory. If they knew what my mission was, I would have arrived at the impact point to find a Russian colonel smugly balancing the chunk of lidanium on his knee. They had warning, all right, but only a few hours' worth. That made the identity of the tipster pretty clear. She had made it quite obvious this time.

There was a spot where my trail ran parallel to the Russians', about half a mile from it, for quite some distance before turning south to meet it. I stopped the cycle, jammed the accelerator on medium throttle so it would sound like I was working my way up the trail toward the crossing, then took off at a jog cross-country.

NINETEEN

The terrain was like the rest, rolling hills, parallel to the two trails, with tree-capped tops a slight thirty feet above the valleys. It was hard running, but good cover. I could still hear the cycle engine roaring away in the background as I dropped to a crouch and peered over the last of the hills.

The widened trail was clear through the underbrush, and seemingly uninhabited. I dropped to the ground and crawled down the slope to it, the machine gun at the ready in my hands. The trail was straight at that point and I could see a good distance in both directions. There was nobody to the west, but eastward, where my trail joined theirs, I saw the sun shining off a bit of metal or glass. They *were* waiting for me.

After a moment their engines kicked over and they roared up the trail in search of me. It would all be a footrace from here on, I knew, as I got to my feet, sprinted across the trail and into the woods on the other side. I had no more than a twenty minute jump on them, for once they found the cycle with its jammed accelerator they would figure out I took the shortest possible route—straight overland—to the Amur. But there were no trails anymore, and they would have to cover the distance the same way as me—on foot. Assuming there were no Olympic class runners at the Trygda border outpost, I was pretty safe.

It was three miles to the river. The terrain was the same as before for the first mile, then degenerated into marshland that fortunately was solid enough in spots for me to pick my way through. But it slowed me down, and as a result I didn't find the bank of the Amur until three-quarters of an hour after leaving the Russian trail.

The bank was a series of large, grassy hassocks. Standing on one, I leaned out and looked up and down the Amur. The water was clear to the west, but to the east, around a slight bend in the river, came the chugging of a boat. It would be too much to hope for that it turn out to be a Chinese barge, I knew.

I hid behind a group of reeds and watched as a small Russian patrol boat moved cautiously down my side of the river. It was an old, wooden boat with a lapstrake hull that should have been painted ten years ago. It looked more like the *African Queen* than a military vessel, but the two men standing in the stern, holding RPD's, were impressive enough.

I stood stock-still while the boat passed, hoping it would go far enough to the west to let me swim to the Chinese side. I didn't relish the notion of swimming with twenty pounds of lidanium strapped to my body, but the inflatable boat was miles away and there was certainly no time to look for it. I kicked off my boots, socks and pack, and tied the satchel of lidanium to my belt. I stripped off my jacket and shoulder holster, sticking the Luger in a pants pocket.

The patrol boat went down the river a bit, and turned and came back. It was making short trips over a preset route. There certainly were others like it making similiar runs along that stretch of river bank where I was expected to surface. The effort to catch me was shaping up to be bigger than anything I expected.

There was no time to wait for the boat to pass, especially since it would be upon me again before I could swim halfway across the river. I aimed the machine gun and waited. The two gunmen had switched sides of the boat so they could keep a sharp eye on the shoreline. The pilot was partly obscured from view, standing in a four-by-four pilothouse with windows on three sides.

The patrol boat was but thirty feet from shore, and the men on it impossible to miss. God, but I hated to do it that way. Realizing they wouldn't have the same reticence, I opened fire. One short burst swept both gunmen from the deck and tossed them into the murky water, dead before they hit. The pilot panicked, swung the bow away from shore and shoved the throttle all the way forward. I saw him reach for his radio, and I turned the RPD on him.

Slugs ripped the pilothouse to shreds, blew out all the windows and toppled the radio antenna until its shining metal tip dragged in the Amur. I aimed for the transom, for the fuel tanks, and sent a long burst into them until they blew up in a glorious fury of white-and-yellow fire. The old boat was ripped half apart and the shock wave from the blast whipped the reeds in which I hid.

The boat churned straight across the river and sank a third of the way out from the Chinese side, leaving only the topmost part of the pilothouse above water. I threw aside the RPD, dived into the water and swam like crazy.

The lidanium was tied to my belt and hung loosely, not nearly the inconvenience I had imagined. But the current was swift and a wind was rippling the water. I had to keep looking up to get my bearings, and what I was hearing and seeing wasn't good. The buzz of boat propellers was drawing nearer—another patrol boat, maybe two. And overhead, the beating of a helicopter rotor was sadly unmistakable.

The propeller noise was now close enough for me to distinguish two boats, and I could feel the toro wash from the helicopter beating down the waves around me. An amplified voice yelled at me in Russian, then English, but I couldn't make out the words. I was swimming much too fast for that; nearly on top of the sunken hulk of the old patrol boat, a third of the way out from the Chinese side. I looked up to see one of the newly arrived boats pull in front of me. My hand touched the side of the boat I had sent to the bottom. I stopped swimming.

"Do not try to escape," the amplified voice boomed in English that was quite clear this time.

I was right next to the sunken boat in ten feet of clear water. I dropped a hand to my waist, untied the sock holding the lidanium to my belt and let it drop.

"Stay still," the voice said.

"Sure, sure," I grumbled to myself, and held on to the sunken hulk until I was pulled aboard one of the Russian boats.

The Russian border outpost of Trygda looked as if it were on the edge of the world. The camp—it could hardly be called a town—consisted largely of a barracks, an operations shack with a fifty-foot radio antenna atop it, two short docks and an assortment of utility buildings. A single rail line disappeared to the northeast, to hook up with the Trans-Siberian tracks at Belogorsk, ninety miles away. Wherever they kept the airstrip it was not to be seen.

The men on the boat said nothing to me all the way to Trygda, but at no time were fewer than three guns trained on me. They gave me a cursory pat-down, but found only the Luger. Hugo, my stiletto, and Pierre, my gas bomb went undetected. It was rocky in the boat, and wet, and I had the feeling that knowing I had already accounted for a platoon of their comrades made them somewhat unwilling to get close.

At Trygda I was taken off the boat and marched to the door of the operations shack, a one-story structure to which several additions had been attached and which had come to resemble a cheap American tract home. They didn't have handcuffs on the boat, so I had my hands in my pockets when they marched me up to the shack.

A Russian colonel stood in the door, tapping his fingers casually upon the leather flap covering his belt holster. He wore knee-high leather boots outside his uniform trousers, and reminded me of a Tartar George Patton. He smirked when I was stood in front of him.

"Welcome to Trygda, Mr. Carter," he said.

"My pleasure. Is Rita here yet?"

He was startled for a moment, then leaned his head back and roared with laughter. "So . . . the little viper with whom I have been saddled all day is not so clever as she thinks! That *is* good news. It almost makes up for your decimating my patrol force. Yes, Mr. Carter, she is here at the moment . . . inside, preparing to relish your surprise upon seeing her."

"Let's not disappoint the lady," I said.

"No, we must not do that. Come inside. You will behave, won't you? I don't want to have a man of your eminence trussed up—at least not with a lady present."

"I'll behave."

"Good. In you go."

The colonel pushed open the door and stepped inside, and as he did so his laughter returned. When I got into the small office and my eyes adjusted to the light, I saw Rita sitting on his desk. She was wearing a pair of leather pants, but her triumph had been spoiled, and anger was creeping across her once-beautiful face.

"My dear Miss Brennan," the colonel went on gleefully, "I'm afraid that your victim anticipated you. He asked if you were here."

"I don't believe it," she said, outraged and astonished.

"It's true. Since Andrea knew exactly where I was going, the colonel would have been waiting for me at the impact point had she given me away. That was hardly the case."

"The impact point?" the colonel asked. "What is the impact point?"

"See what I mean. The impact point, colonel, is a spot in the woods about ten miles from here where we thought one of our spy satellites had gone down. I was sent to recover anything important which might have survived.''

"A spy satellite? In our woods?"

"And why not. One fell in Canada some years ago, and of course Skylab went down over southwest Australia. It's hardly unheard of.''

"This satellite . . . did you find it?"

"I found an impact point. If it *was* our satellite, nothing identifiable remains. It's my opinion the fallen object was a meteorite and that, once again, the big brains in the Pentagon have goofed. I can translate that last phrase into Russian if you like.''

"I know what it means," he replied tersely.

"You can't make me believe I trailed you halfway around the world for a goddamn meteorite," Rita exploded.

"What's the matter?" I asked. "Afraid Moscow won't take kindly to your squandering the budget chasing me around for nothing?"

The colonel smiled and looked away so Rita couldn't see it. Whether she was home-grown or a Western convert, Rita must have had enough clout in the Kremlin so he couldn't be *too* openly scornful of her. His reaction increased her importance as a target for me by several notches. That is, assuming I lived to go around picking my targets. That possibility was getting more doubtful by the minute.

"I watched you, Carter," she hissed. "I watched you in Scotland—"

"You weren't there," I cut in.

"No, but friends were. And I arranged meeting you in New York.''

"It occurred to me as a possibility. Are *they* here, too?"

Rita seemed to blush, then regained her composure. She was not as cool as she thought. It's good Moscow is getting their use out of her while she's young, I thought, for she will never see middle age.

"Moscow *wants* you," she said.

"Oh, *that's* a secret."

"And they felt if I could get to tag along with you on a mission . . . especially one so close to the border—"

"You'd have earned your keep. Well, you did your job. I crossed the border and they got me. Why don't you give us the obligatory speech about how much you hated going to bed with me, and then leave. I'm sick of looking at you."

Rita's face turned beet red. She crossed the room, slapped my face and said to the colonel, "I'll need a boat back to the Chinese side. I have to be back at the expedition's camp before sunset so I can play the role of the distressed girlfriend whose man is missing."

The colonel nodded, and waved to a functionary to take care of her. When she was gone, he sighed. "My God, I don't know how you put up with her."

TWENTY

"She has certain talents," I said.

"I suppose you are right. She is a beautiful woman."

"Russian-born, of course?"

"No. A Finn. I am Russian. My name is Sergei Yudenich. I am a colonel in the regular army. This impact zone . . . I will have to see it."

"The map is in my pocket. May I get it?"

"Of course."

I took out the soggy piece of plasticized paper, unfolded it and laid out my entire route for the man. There was no point in not doing it. He had a fair idea of where I was anyway, from simply following the trail of bodies.

He studied the map for a time, then shrugged. "There were reports of lightning and a forest fire in that region a while ago. Nothing was thought of it. You *are* telling the truth, aren't you. You realize there's no point in lying now."

"I'm not lying. There is a region of devastation where the object impacted and no evidence of a satellite. I dug for one—you will find evidence of that—but found nothing to indicate a satellite.''

"You found nothing at all?''

"Rocks . . . ashes . . . no satellite. The idiots at the Pentagon must have been wrong. See for yourself.''

"I will, Mr. Carter, I will. We will go there and see if what you say is true. You will stay here. I would like to offer you hospitality, but I'm afraid the matter is out of my hands.''

"I didn't expect a state visit,'' I said.

"I'm afraid you will not get one. There are two men from the KGB here to speak with you. I can give you time to build up your strength first, if you like.''

"No. Let's get on with it.''

"As you wish. I would like to shake your hand. Your reputation is well-known and, I'm afraid to say, well-founded. But to do so would be hypocritical. Goodbye, Mr. Carter.''

And he was gone. I was left with three Red Army guards who, without any expression, pushed me through a back door. I was shoved through a dark and musty file room into the last addition to the building, a storage area devoid of anything but wooden crates, cobwebs and a few steel uprights. The room was dark but for a bare bulb hanging from the ceiling; the two small windows were covered over with newspaper. The crates bore Russian and East German markings listing assorted dried fruits and vegetables, and canned meat.

The Russians tied me to one of the uprights, using quarter-inch nylon line, then left me alone. They fixed the rope around my wrists, missing the sheath for Hugo by two inches. They left my legs untied. There was nothing for me to do with them other than hold myself up, and my KGB interrogators certainly would not be detained by their freedom.

I was alone in the dark for less than twenty minutes. The door opened and two men entered. It was the two I expected, the tall man and the short one I fought on that deserted street in New York. They said nothing, but stood in front of me, glaring at me, a clear vision of vengeance in their eyes. The short one had his mouth wired, a remnant of the time I caved in his jaw, and could hardly speak. He didn't need to; I knew well enough what was coming next.

"I had to come all the way to Siberia to run into two New York City muggers," I said.

The tall one scowled at me, and said, "You will tell us why you are here."

"I told the colonel."

"Tell us."

I sighed. "I was sent to look for an American spy satellite which re-entered the atmosphere and crashed a few miles from here. There was nothing left of it. Your comrades caught me on the way back to China."

"You lie," the big one said, and his smaller companion grunted evilly.

"What can I tell you, pal?" I shrugged. "You're not going to believe me, no matter what I say."

"Tell the truth."

"On one condition."

"And what is that?"

"You talk first. Tell me why Rita and you were after me in New York."

They looked at one another, conferred silently, until the big one said, in Russian, "There's no reason not to tell him."

To me he spoke in English: "It wasn't just New York. We picked you up in Scotland."

"In Scotland, I was in a small town. I would have seen you there."

"It happened in Glasgow. You were identified by our resident agent, and we were given the word to follow you. The woman was assigned to make contact, which we arranged in New York."

"Yeah, and I bet you're really thrilled you did it. Tell me

. . . what was I doing that caused you to be assigned to me? My work in Scotland had nothing to do with Mother Russia.''

The tall man laughed roughly. ''We were interested in you on general principle. I wanted to kill you right away, but Moscow said 'no . . . follow him . . . insinuate a woman into his confidence'.''

''She was into a good deal more than that,'' I said.

The Russian didn't understand me, and shrugged. ''Your turn now,'' he said. ''Tell us the truth.''

''You're not going to like it.''

''I don't like it already.''

''I came here looking for what my people thought might be a downed satellite. If that's what it was, it was totally destroyed in the impact. Personally, I think the thing was an asteroid and my people were wrong. Colonel Yudenich has gone to look for it. Ask him when he gets back.''

''We will,'' the man replied.

He turned away from me, exchanged more pregnant glances with his companion, then at an unspoken signal the small man was unleashed. He whirled at me, driving a fist into my stomach. I wasn't ready and the blow doubled me over. The little man's face nearly twisted into a smile, despite the wires lacing up his jaw. His companion aimed a right at my jaw. I took it, and rolled with it, snapping my head to one side, then slumping to the floor.

It seemed like a good idea to pretend the lights had gone out for a while. It was. They kicked idly at my boots, then left me alone, locking the door behind them.

The two KGB men shut off the light when they left, and what little sunlight there was trickled in a muted gray through the papered-over windows. The pain in my gut went away after a time, as did the nausea that always went with being popped in the stomach. I faked unconsciousness not just to avoid being hit more, but to buy time. It would take Yudenich the rest of the daylight hours to verify my story about the impact point. And he would *have* to verify it. The beauty of my story was that there was no way the Russians could trip me up on it. Not that it mattered much; they had more than enough reason to set me up in front of a pine tree and shoot me. I had, after all, killed a good number of their men.

I needed the extra time to figure out a means of escape and the hours of darkness to do it in.

The nylon line binding my wrists was quarter-inch twisted rope, of the sort that stretched ten feet in every hundred. It was also of cheap manufacture and loose twist. I worked at it until one wrist was free enough to allow me to snap Hugo into place.

The razor-sharp stiletto sliced through one strand of the line with ease, and I simply maintained pressure until the whole damn thing unravelled. I was free.

I got to my feet and checked the door. It was locked all right, and from the front room I could hear the voices of two guards talking in Russian, discussing a soccer match.

The paper on the windows pried loose easily enough. In the fading daylight, I could tell that the outpost was largely deserted, Yudenich apparently having taken a sizeable contingent of men with him to the impact site. An old sidecar motorcycle stood against a tree a few yards from the shack where I was being held.

I looked around the storage room which was my temporary prison. There was a thousand-foot roll of quarter-inch nylon, the same rope with which I had been bound. I cut off a four-foot length and left it by the post to which I was tethered, in case it was later necessary to pretend I was still tied up.

I checked out the supplies piled high in the room. There were candles, and canned food of various kinds—dried meat and stewed vegetables, principally beets, carrots and cabbage. The cases had never been opened. Even at a remote border outpost, I thought, the Russians have taste.

There were four five-gallon jugs of kerosene used in powering the hurricane lamps I had seen hanging in various strategic spots. Apparently, the Russian power system was unreliable. The kerosene interested me more than did the canned goods. I uncorked two jugs and placed them in precarious balance atop one pile of boxes. I left the corks in loosely so the fumes would not escape and alert the guards in the other room. But I tied a ten-foot length of nylon line to their handles, and ran it across the room. I tied the other end to the doorknob. If anyone opened the door, the jugs would be toppled to the floor and break, where I lit a candle and left it waiting for them.

I figured I had two hours before Yudenich came back and I was checked on. I opened a can of dried beef and, sitting on a stack of rations, picked at it with the tip of my knife.

TWENTY-ONE

Darkness fell quickly, the long shadows of late afternoon turning to the gray of twilight and, at last, the black of the Siberian night. As the light waned, so did the temperature, until the few men at the border outpost save the sentry were indoors. The barracks windows were clouded with condensation, but through them I could see the occasional outlines of men walking idly around.

I figured that Trygda had a standing complement of only about twenty men, half of whom went with Yudenich to the impact site. There were one, perhaps two, guarding me. I presumed that my "friends" from New York were in the barracks with everyone else. It was time to move.

I opened the window as wide as it would go and took a long look outside. As before, there was no one to be seen; it was, I imagined, chow time. I could hear men's voices, and the sound of a radio. I rolled up a piece of paper that I had torn from the window, and set fire to it. Then I gave a sharp tug on the rope I tied to the kerosene jugs. The heavy glass containers crashed to the floor, shattering and sending their contents flying across the room.

Within ten seconds, two guards crashed through the door into the room, machine guns at the ready. I tossed my flaming paper torch into the center of the room and dived out the window.

It wasn't a loud explosion, just a low *whump* which shook the walls of the frame building and blew out the windows. A jet of flame licked at my feet as I went out the window, hit the ground and rolled to come up in a crouch with my knife in my hand. There were screams and a man burst out the front door of the operations shack, his clothes on fire.

I ran across the dirt road separating the shack from the barracks and dropped to my knees behind a short, fat spruce.

The man who had the bad luck to burst into the bomb I prepared for him was running in circles, slapping his hands at his face and clothes, the fire searing his skin until it peeled off in long, sickly strips. His comrade was luckier. He never made it out of the building.

The barracks emptied, some men running to help their flaming countryman, others dashing in the front door of the operations shack, presumably in an attempt to contain the fire. I counted eight. Allowing for one or two sentries, that would give me about ten more Russians to deal with. And, of course, there were those out in the field with Yudenich.

As if on cue, every single man came out of the barracks, leaving me free to go in the back door. It was a large room. The munitions closet was locked, but only with a quarter-inch bolt padlock. My knife wouldn't pry it open, but it only took half a minute to find a screwdriver that would. Men who are careful to keep their guns locked up can always be relied upon to leave hefty screwdrivers, hammers, pliers and other suitable burglar's tools lying around on tabletops.

I snapped the lock plate from the jamb and pulled open the door. Outside, there was much shouting and small explosions as cans of provisions superheated and blew up. Even the crackling of the flames was deafening as the fire quickly enveloped the entire operations building. There was what sounded like a hose being turned on.

The munitions closet held a few dozen various-sized weapons and two crates of grenades. I took an automatic pistol, an automatic rifle and as many grenades as I could stuff into my pockets. Then I pulled the pin on one grenade, tossed the pint-sized bomb into the munitions locker and ran like hell.

For the second time in five minutes, a building at the Trygda base went up in smoke. The munitions closet went up in one big explosion and a series of tiny ones. First, the crates of grenades detonated. Then, the handgun and rifle ammunition ignited, creating a massive and deadly fireworks display. Fire went straight up to the ceiling and, from there, sideways until the entire roof was engulfed. I stood behind a back corner of the building and waited until three or four Russians, bewildered by the total assault on their compound, stumbled tentatively toward what remained of their barracks. I stepped out from behind the corner then, and poured half a clip of bullets into them. They dropped where they stood dead too fast to be surprised.

The shoulder weapon I snatched from the Russian locker was a 7.62mm AK with a thirty-two shot magazine. I had about half the first magazine left, and the entire second firmly tucked under my belt. I shifted to the other side of the barracks, which was pressed into the woods and harder to travel along. Thorns and other underbrush crept up the side of the building, but I had been through so much that it hardly mattered.

When I reached the front of the barracks, the operations shack was entirely in flames and beyond rescue. The man I set on fire was a blackened corpse lying on the dark Siberian earth. The fire hose was out, the building abandoned to the fire. The half-dozen Russian troops who remained at the base were nowhere to be seen. I knew they had gone either in search of weapons or to guard the border, probably both. The two men I had grappled with in New York were also gone. That bothered me most of all, because I knew those two guys had a long-standing personal grudge against me and were not bound by the customary constraints of military conduct.

I stepped out from behind the shelter of the barracks wall. It was just as well, for that building was well on its way toward incineration. I had to make it to the river, so I skirted the woods in that direction. Staying in the shadows at the edge where the cleared portion of the camp met the forest, I got within a hundred yards of the Amur before I saw them. Worse, *they* saw *me*.

The half-dozen men I couldn't locate near the buildings had run to the boats, where they kept a supply of arms. They knew I would head in that direction and were waiting for me.

Russian machine gun slugs tore up the ground at my feet as I dived into the woods yet another time. I rolled and came up firing, finishing the second half of the clip without any real idea whether I hit anyone.

By now, the boats would be deployed and any hope of getting the chance to swim over to the Chinese side was gone, at least for a while. I counted to five and leaped to my feet, taking off across the base at a sprint.

They didn't expect that. They thought I would head for the river or into the woods, not run north back in the direction of the burning buildings and darkest Siberia.

I ran between the hulks of the operations shack and barracks, vaulting the burned body which lay between them. As I ran, I threw away the spent cartridge and shoved my backup cartridge into the body of the machine gun. My unexpected action may have thrown the Russians off, but not so much as to prevent their pegging a few rounds in my direction. They did not, however, give chase, at least not right away. Apparently they felt that guarding the border was more important than running after me. They may have been right. I sure as hell didn't plan to spend the rest of my life hiding out in the forests of Siberia. Sooner or later, I would have to attempt a border crossing, and they would be waiting.

I picked up the single-track railroad which eventually joined the Trans-Siberian and followed it as far as the Trygda airstrip.

The airstrip was as rudimentary as the one at Aihui, perhaps more so. It was unkindly hacked out of the forest which just as rudely kept intruding back upon it. The only building was a pilot's shack half the size of the first building I torched on the base proper. Lights were on inside it, but no one seemed to be outside, and no planes were on the airstrip.

I knew better than to go running up on the assumption there was nobody home. My two mugger friends from New York were still among the missing, for one thing. It would have been nice to find a simple two-seater transport sitting on the strip with the keys still in the ignition. In that case, I might have taken a chance. But the only vehicle within sight was one of the Russians' ubiquitous motorcycles, this one without a sidecar. It rested up against a slender pine ten yards from the pilot's shcak.

A group of slim, thirty-year-old pitch pines made up that section of forest behind the shack. I crept around to it, and from there stepped to the rear wall of the shack. There was no sound from within. The possibility that the men in it had run to investigate the fires on the main base was tempting. I pressed an ear to the wall, but heard nothing.

Through a crack between the old, weathered boards I also saw nothing. I went to the only door, which faced the runway, and went inside.

The pilots' shack looked like any such building Marine fliers put up on islands all over the Pacific during the Second World War. It was square, with old chairs, the stuffing of which hung in strips and chunks to the floor; a card table upon which sat a half-empty bottle of vodka and several glasses, and an ashtray filled to the rim with the stubs of Balkan cigarettes; a couch as old as the chairs, some straight-back chairs, a smaller table and two cabinets. The top of one cabinet held more vodka and glasses even dirtier than the first. The top of the other held radio equipment, tuned to the local military aviation frequency. It was the only radio I had seen on the base, which appeared to have no telephones. I pulled the cord from the back of the set and, as an added measure, stuck my knife into the guts of the transceiver and twisted it around. There would be no way of repairing that baby, at least not on an overnight basis.

I searched the rooms. There were creature comforts, but no weapons. Russian aeronautical charts of the Trygda region were twenty years old and had the airfield penciled in. Assorted flares, tools and functional items like wire and tape filled several drawers. On the card table, a Russian soldier had nearly finished writing a letter to his sweetheart in Leningrad on the back of a snapshot of himself and two friends.

I headed for the exit, the solitary door facing the airstrip, but it opened first. A man pushed his way in, an automatic pistol at the ready. He was followed by another, shorter man, whose orthopedic patchwork identified him clearly.

They had me, but good. I dropped my guns.

TWENTY-TWO

''We thought you come this way,'' the tall one, the only one of the pair who seemed able to speak, said. ''Soldiers say you go toward river. We say you go here.''

''Good for you, buster,'' I replied.

''Empty pockets.''

I did as I was told, dumping the spare cartridges on the floor beside the two guns and the hand grenades I had stolen.

''You be careful what you do. We are not stupid, like the army idiots. They do not even know how to bind a man's arms.''

''No doubt you do. Do you guys have names, by the way?''

''Names are of no importance to us. You, on the other hand, are important man. You deserve your reputation.''

''You wouldn't say that if you were in the army,'' I replied.

''They are idiots,'' the Russian said, spitting on the floor to strengthen his point.

"What beat do you guys walk? I mean, where is your normal assignment? United States?"

"Western Europe."

"This is kind of out of the way for you, isn't it?"

"It is the end of the earth. Which is why we are eager to leave, even though it means taking you with us."

I was not really surprised. They had the time to call the office for instructions, and Moscow doubtlessly realized I was worth more alive than dead.

"You will come with us to Moscow. It will be a long trip, by jeep and then by train, and we will allow no more escapes. This time you will be suitably bound. First, you will be properly searched. Take off your clothes, all of them."

I shrugged and unbuckled my belt. "This is gonna be a ball," I said, and reaching into my pants, plucked from under my scrotum Pierre, the tiny gas bomb I kept taped to my thigh.

I tossed it onto the floor, then dived to my right to escape any bullets the Russian might instinctively hurl in my direction. I knew he wouldn't kill me if he didn't have too. He had so kindly provided me with the knowledge that Moscow wanted me alive. It was his instincts that worried me. I needen't have bothered. He controlled his instincts well. It killed him.

As the two of them recoiled from Pierre's noxious fumes, I clicked my stiletto into place and, lunging forward, drove it into the tall one's chest.

The blade entered just under and to the right of the sternum. I dragged it across his chest, making a three-inch slit in the man's middle and halving his heart as if it were a round of cheese. He stared at me with eyes as fixed as gum balls, blood soaking his shirt and jacket until he dropped, as dead as they come.

The short one whose jaw I rearranged some weeks earlier was without weapons; transfixed for a moment, then stumbling to avoid Pierre's gas, he was open for a setup. I gave him one: a left to the gut followed by a right cross to the chin.

He spun, coughing from the gas. I thought he was on the way out, I was wrong. In a move I hadn't thought him capable of, my short adversary produced a tiny pistol from an inside pocket.

The pistol was a derringer or the Russian equivalent of one; a two-shot, over-and-under waistcoat pocket arm suitable more for a woman than a man. As he produced it, the Russian lowered his head, part of a general body move to conceal the weapon until it was ready to be fired.

I was too fast for him. I swept up with Hugo, driving the stiletto straight into the Russian's left eye. The man hung on the point of my knife for an instant, yellow and red fluids sleeking down over my fist, until the blade twisted round in his brain and brought him slowly to the floor.

I shook the debris off my hand, then wiped my hand on his pants.

I kicked open the door and went outside, wiping my eye to remove the sting of the gas and edging back around to the rear of the building. No one else had come. In their disdain for the Red Army soldiers, my two KGB friends had neglected to tell anyone about having captured me. I was alone, at least for now.

After taking five minutes to let the gas clear out of the pilots' shack, I went back inside for my weapons. I crammed my pockets full one more time, then scrounged around until I found two cans of gas meant for the motorcycle parked outside. I emptied one five-gallon tin on the floor and spilled the contents of the other around the propane tanks behind the shack used to fuel the small furnace. Then I tossed a grenade through a window and ran like hell to where the motorcycle stood. The building didn't just explode—it seemed to disintegrate. The walls blew apart, one plank separating from another, the whole thing collapsing into a gigantic bonfire. I got onto the cycle and kicked over the engine.

It wasn't that I had a need to destroy *every* building at

Trygda, although that wasn't a bad thought. Basically, I
wanted to draw as many Russian soldiers from the banks of
the Amur as I could. That was shaping up to be a pretty tough
problem; from the east, I heard the roar and saw the lights of a
caravan of motorcycles. It was Yudenich and his men, returning from the meteorite impact site and heading straight for
me. Instead of one group of Russians chasing me, now I had
two. I took off down the landing strip, toward the far end of
the field, where my memory of the Mukhino map told me a
trail led off into the woods.

The trail was an old one; narrow and largely overgrown
with grass and elk weed. The Siberian reindeer whose hooves
kept open so many trails in that region abandoned this one
when the airstrip was cut. That was fine with me. I wanted
to be alone, preferably with a clear route to the border. I knew
that by following this trail and hooking up with one other, I
would be at the river. Without hesitating, I roared down the
trail, leaving Trygda behind and hoping I had gotten into the
woods before Yudenich and his boys had the chance to see
me.

For a time, I *was* alone. I had to slow to about ten miles an
hour because the trail was so neglected and narrow, but at that
speed I was able to shut off the headlamp and drive by
moonlight.

The trail wound slowly southward, arcing like the one I
tried earlier, before I was captured by the Russians. In taking
it, I was banking on the Russians concentrating their
border-watch around Trygda. I was also counting on their
being so mad at me for having leveled their base that they
would make mistakes.

My recollection of the Mukhino map placed me a mile and
a half from the river, in a section of Siberian forest criss-
crossed with trails, some of them negotiable by motorcycle.

Before me lay terrain on a sharp incline, building up to
cliffs nearly as tall as the ones upon which I found the
paleolithic cave. I took that path because I felt it the one

direction the Russians would be least likely to suspect me of taking. They would expect me to pick the nearest possible section of river bank, I thought, when in reality I would gladly risk a forty-foot drop into the water in exchange for a head start. I didn't want to be caught by patrol boats and helicopters this time.

I switched the headlamp back on and roared southward toward the river. The trail joined a newer, wider one, and my uphill climb became a lot easier. I saw no one else, and planned only for my ejection over the Amur. I knew that the trail dead-ended atop the cliff. I figured if I hit the crest at forty miles-per-hour, I would be carried at least sixty feet out over the river, and jump from the cycle in time to land safely in ten feet of water. From there on, the swim to the other side would be swift and uneventful.

That was the plan. I should have known better than to think it would work. For as I neared a lateral trail that was scarcely a mile from the crest, I was half-blinded by the glare of headlights.

A jeep was parked in the cross-path, as if waiting for me. On hearing the roar of my engine, the driver hit the lights. I was stunned for a second, but kept driving. I whipped the Russian machine gun around, took both hands off the cycle controls and fired a magazine in the direction of the jeep.

I heard a scream, and saw one of the lights go out, before the cycle spun off the trail, hit a fallen branch and flipped over. I jumped off it, tossing the machine gun aside and rolling through yet another briar patch to come up on my feet, the automatic pistol at the ready.

Several long bursts of machine gun fire tore up the bark of a sweet pine to my right and I dropped back to the ground. There was damned little cover in that section of woods, only the underbrush and an occasional pine, most of them too slender to hide a man. But even inadequate cover was preferable to the Russians, who by now could be assumed ready to hang me from the highest tree in Siberia. I lurched up, fired two quick shots at the jeep to keep the gunman's head down, then ran like hell toward a tree fifty yeards away. I got behind it and gritted my teeth as slugs ripped the bark on both sides of me.

Two more quick shots and I was off again. This time I made it nearly a hundred yards, and crossed the trail where the jeep was stationed. I could see the jeep through the bushes, outlined by its own headlight. If there were more than two men left manning that machine gun, I would be surprised. I whipped around the tree trunk, fired a shot at what looked like a head and heard a shriek.

I ran as fast as I could toward the cliff, reloading my pistol as I hurdled logs and skirted especially dense patches of undergrowth.

I heard a voice, and bullets ripped into the bushes around me. I spun, trying desperately to jam the cartridge into the gun, but the Russian automatic stuck. I saw a muzzle flash, and felt a searing pain in my right thigh. The automatic was hopelessly stuck. My leg crumpled beneath me, and I fell to the forest floor.

TWENTY-THREE

Thank God the wound was a clean one. The bullet must have been tipped, for it passed straight through my thigh halfway up from the knee, puncturing two muscles but not demolishing them. I wouldn't be doing much walking for a while, but would suffer no permanent damage. At least, not from that particular wound.

"Turn over," a voice growled. I recognized it as belonging to Yudenich, the Russian base commandant.

I did as I was told, rolling onto my back, holding the wound in my leg to stop the bleeding.

"Hello, colonel," I said. "Did you find the impact zone?"

"I—*I found it*," he said, more in a stammer than a growl, which is how he would have preferred it sound. He was trying to decide whether to follow orders and take me to Moscow, or follow his instincts and shoot me on the spot. The longer I kept him talking, the more chance I had it would be the former. That in turn would give me time to figure out another escape plan. It was clear I wouldn't be doing any more running through the woods for a while.

"Was it like I said?" I asked.

"Yes, it was *like you said*. It appears that a meteorite *did* land in the woods there. Damn it, Carter, you killed twenty of my men!"

"Everyone has a bad day now and then," I joked, trying to keep my spirits up.

"My base! Trygda is practically destroyed! I did not believe such a thing was possible for one man. Tell me you had others with you, there were comrades who escaped. I want to hear it."

"If it makes you happy," I said, tearing the left sleeve off my shirt and wrapping it around the wound in my leg.

Yudenich stepped back a few paces and sat on the stump of an old pine blown down by a long-ago storm.

"It is incredible. I go away for a few hours, and look what happens. Surely there were others with you. American—or Chinese—I do not care."

"Okay, colonel," I said with a sigh. "Make your report out to read that Trygda was leveled by a sneak attack by the perfidious Chinese. Just leave me out of it."

"How can I leave you out of it?" he shot back. "You must go to Moscow, with me, to explain."

"I don't think that will be good for your career, and maybe not for your health," I said. "Imagine yourself explaining how one lone American killed most of your men and destroyed Trygda. Better it was done by a Chinese platoon. It will seem like just another skirmish."

"The Chinese will deny it."

"Of course. They will deny anything your government accuses them of, including their obvious backing of my mission here."

Yudenich nodded reluctantly.

"Moscow expects a denial from Peking. Moscow probably even expects a Chinese-provoked border incident. What Moscow *doesn't* expect is having to listen to Colonel Yudenich explain how one lone American made a shambles of Trygda."

Yudenich was silent for a long time, then said, almost whining, "You know, Mr. Carter, I had a promising career at one time."

"You still have one, if you listen to me."

"I come from an eminent family, did you know that? But I worked long and hard in the army, and it was forgiven me." He laughed a bitter laugh. "This assignment . . . it was to be the first step up into the hierarchy. Instead it is my last, and all because of an American agent who now has the temerity to demand I let him go."

"Not demand. I'm in no position to make demands. I'm simply asking you to accept the logic of your situation. Moscow won't believe you if you haul me in and point the finger at me. They'll think it was the Chinese platoon, no matter what you say. Only they'll think you are either mad or in some way a traitor. Let me go, colonel. It's your only hope. I can make it across the Amur on my own."

"No, you can't. It's heavily patrolled now. I put all my men along it in boats, and I've called in others."

"Let me worry about that," I said.

"No!" Yudenich said, snapping to his feet and waving the muzzle of his machine gun at my belly. "I have made up my mind. You will go with me to Moscow, and we both will, as you say, face the music. My men are coming now. Listen."

There was the sound of far-off motorcycles. He must have called in the few troops that remained at Trygda.

"Get to your feet," Yudenich ordered. "I'm sorry to make you walk on your bad leg, but I won't be the fool my men were and let you get anywhere near me. At the slightest improper move, I will kill you. Is that clear?"

I shrugged and got to my knees, then my feet. It wasn't easy, but I was able to put pressure on my right leg; *walking*, I didn't know about.

The sound of the motorcycles drew nearer. I took a step, and stumbled. True to his word, Yudenich's hands tensed around the rifle. I could almost feel the pressure on the trigger. Then there was a shot, a single sharp crack made by a weapon of smaller caliber than the Russian gun.

Yudenich stiffened and his arms twitched, tossing the machine gun to one side. Then he clutched his chest and slid straight down to his knees. He hovered there for a second, then fell onto his side, dead.

The shot that killed him came from my left. I looked there, and saw an amazing sight. Andrea Regan stood by a small pine, a hunting rifle clenched tightly in her hands, still aimed at the spot where Yudenich so recently stood.

Andrea's eyes were wide and fixed on me. She looked paralyzed, like a statue. Beside her was the old Indian, Setka. He smiled faintly at me, then pried the rifle from her white-knuckled hands and dropped it onto the ground.

I hobbled toward Andrea and nearly fell, the pain in my leg weakening me. Surprised out of her state of shock, Andrea ran to me, wrapped her arms around me and silently helped me to stand.

"Nice shot," I said. "What the hell are you doing in Siberia?"

"I followed Rita. Did you know the second you left camp this morning she was up and following you?"

"I was told later on."

"She was dressed and waiting for you . . . thought I was asleep, too. My intelligence was insulted. So I pulled on my clothes and went after her. A *Russian boat* took her across the Amur!"

"That must have been a shocker."

"I swam across, followed her as far as I could, and then met these fellows. This man appears to be a friend of yours."

She motioned to Setka, who came up quickly.

"We must go," he said in Mandarin. "The motorbikes are coming."

That fact was fairly inescapable, for the sound was no more than a mile off now.

"Where are we going to hide, Setka?" I asked. "There isn't much cover, and I'm afraid I've run my last marathon for a while."

"Follow me," he said, then turned without another word and walked briskly to the west, in the direction of a large stand of medium-sized spruce.

I took a step and winced in pain.

Andrea slid under my right arm and took the weight off my leg. We tried to approximate a jog, but it was impossible. It was like the old three-legged race; difficult to learn and impossible to carry out.

The motors drew nearer. Setka yelled something in Mukhino, and in a flash two burley Indians ran out from beneath the cover of the spruce trees. They took me by the arms and, without a word being exchanged, I was carried into a safe hiding spot.

TWENTY-FOUR

The spruce grove was near the top of a stretch of land which sloped down at a fairly steep angle, ending in a seasonal stream which fed, ultimately, into the Amur. The slope sheltered much of the grove from the view of persons on the flatland above, and in it the Mukhinos had tethered four horses. They were dray horses, bred for pulling carts halfway across the Chinese and Siberian countryside, not speed. But at that point, with my leg feeling the way it was, they were better than nothing.

The two Indians who were helping me walk hoisted me onto the back of a dapple gray mare. Andrea hopped up behind me and, putting her arms around me, rested a cheek on my shoulder.

"I killed a man," she said.

Setka pulled his horse alongside mine, then told me to follow him. "We are going to the stream bed, then north two miles, and east three miles. Follow us."

I knew better than to argue. It was his terrain, not mine,

and any man that certain of his plan under such circumstances must have had a good one. I waited for the three other horses to start off, then lined up behind them. The sound of the Russian motorcycles was near, but to no avail. They would have to search a square mile of trails and underbrush before looking down past the spruce grove, and we would be long gone by then.

"I killed a man, " Andrea repeated.

"Welcome to the world."

"What do you mean?"

"I mean that life isn't as simple and clean as they tell you in graduate school. Normally, the killing is done by people like me and few hear of it. This time, a civilian got involved. You saved my life, you know."

Andrea said nothing, which I took to be a denial.

"You really did," I said. "I won't lie and tell you that I might not have gotten away if you hadn't shown up, but you sure as hell made things easier."

"Paul . . . I mean Nick . . ."

"How did you learn to shoot like that?" I asked.

"I told you . . . I was raised in and around woods. I used to hunt with my father. I never shot anything bigger than a duck. Now to have killed a man . . ."

"A run-of-the-mill Russian colonel who would have been shot by his own people within a month anyway."

"He was a *human being*! I *knew* you were involved in espionage," she went on, "and I tried to deny *I* was involved. But I was. From the moment I knew AXE was funding the expedition, I was involved. And I was jealous of Rita, too. When I saw her betraying you, I couldn't stand it. I followed her. And here I am."

Our horse was traversing a patch of land heavily strewn with rocks and logs. The ride was abruptly rough, and Andrea clung to me more tightly.

As she pulled me against her, I reached back and patted her behind. "I suspected you, at first," I told her.

"I was wondering about that."

"Your meeting with that Chinese man, in San Francisco."

"What?" she asked, astonished.

"On the fringe of Chinatown. I was ordering take-out food. You talked with a young Oriental, and gave him something."

"I gave fifty cents to a Chinese panhandler," she laughed.

"Who then ran away when he thought I was a cop," I said, shaking my head, but grinning.

"I don't believe you chased a panhandler around Chinatown thinking he was a spy."

"It happens to the best of us."

"And the guy who shot at us on the freighter? Which side was he on?"

"A rough guess would be Chinese."

"But why? They're on our side."

"That, Dr. Regan, was the subject of some discussion early on in this mission. I was never in favor of trusting the Chinese, but I got outvoted. Why do you think they might have tried to shoot you on the freighter?" she asked.

"I suppose they had the idea they knew enough about the mission to take over on their own. All they had to do was shoot me and steal the maps from my room."

"If they tried and failed on the boat, why would the Chinese go ahead and treat you well once you landed? Why not keep trying to kill you?"

"The rape attempt on you might have been at least partially an attempt to trap me. It *did* happen rather conveniently under my nose. On the other hand, you *do* have a way of attracting the attention of men."

"Thanks," she said dryly.

"One problem with a scenario wherein the Chinese have been trying to kill me is that we can safely assume they'll keep trying, and I mean once we get back to their side of the river."

"Jesus, that's a real cheery prospect, Nick."

"Yeah, tell me about it. I'm just crazy about the notion of having spent all day getting my ass shot off by the Russians just so the Chinese can have a turn doing the same thing. Let's pretend the other scenario is the right one."

"What's that?"

"That's where the *Russians* tried to have *you* knocked off so Rita wouldn't have competition."

"I like that one better. At least we'll be safe when we get to the Chinese side."

"Rita did seem kind of irritated that she didn't know why I was here."

"Why *are* you here?" Andrea asked.

I was a bit surprised, considering she made such a point of not wanting to know when we first met. "I thought you weren't interested."

"I wasn't. But, my God, Nick, I believe I can be considered involved now."

"I found a chunk of blue-gray metal," I said.

"Metal? What kind of metal?"

"Lidanium."

"The rare element? It exists only in the lab."

"It exists *mostly* in the lab. It also can be found in deep-space meteorites, one of which impacted not far from here."

"Did you find it?" she asked.

"The meteorite, but not the lidanium." I had two reasons for lying. One was that if Andrea was being straight with me, it would keep her fairly safe should we fall into Russian hands. The other was that if I was being double-crossed by yet another woman, the lie might help keep *me* safe. I didn't really believe Andrea was double-crossing me, but with the stakes being what they were I wasn't ruling anything out.

"You came all the way around the world, and went through all this aggravation, to find a chunk of metal?" Andrea asked.

"To *not* find it would be more accurate."

"What's so important about it? From what I recall, it's only value is that it raises the curiosity of scientists."

"Beats me," I replied. "When we get back home, I'll put your question through channels."

Andrea seemed annoyed that I couldn't or wouldn't answer her.

"Come on, Nick," she said. "Do you mean to tell me you don't *care* to know what lidanium does that makes it so valuable."

"I only follow orders," I replied, faking a German accent.

"You're not going to tell me, are you?"

"I'm not a scientist. If you don't know what the stuff does, go look it up. Once we get back to civilization, that is."

She was quiet for a time, not mollified but quiet, then asked, "*Will* we get back to civilization?"

"Sure. There's all kinds of civilization. Washington's. Moscow's. Peking's. I can pretty well guarantee we'll end up in one of 'em."

"Wonderful," Andrea said, then fell silent as the tiny caravan snaked through the woods, drawing nearer to the Mukhino camp.

It was small, a secondary camp used by the tribe when, for various reasons, its main camp north of the Amur was unavailable. We entered a grove surrounded by tall, fat spruce whose canopy provided shelter from all but the closest search.

A dozen Indians wandered over, all smiles and familiarity. We dismounted. Setka came over, and the pressure of having to escape removed, pumped my hand furiously.

"I watched the fires. I knew it was Trygda. I knew you did it. It was a beautiful sight."

"Thanks. You did something fairly nice for me, too."

"It was nothing. I found your friend in the woods and brought her to you. She is a better shot than I am. I don't even have a gun."

"I stole it from the Chinese guards," Andrea explained.

Setka put a bony old arm around my shoulders. "You come to my tent. I have deer stew and black tea. Lots of both.

I look at your leg. I have medicine.''

"Are we safe here?" I asked.

"Of course. Otherwise, I not bring you here. The Russians not even know where camp is, and not think of it anyway. We keep out of the dogs' way.''

"Exactly where are we, Setka?"

"Two miles from river. Seven miles north of Trygda. Not far from where you crossed into Russian territory.''

"And not far from where I sank the Russian patrol boat,'' I mused, thinking of the chunk of lidanium I deep-sixed next to it.

The old man called for help and two brawny tribesmen helped me to his tent.

TWENTY-FIVE

The old man dressed my wounds using a combination of native medicines and antibiotics bought in the trading station at Aihui. I was plied with honey-laced black tea until it was coming out of my ears, and slept for an hour. When I awoke, I was alone in Setka's tent, lying on a soft bed of pine needles covered with discarded cloth. Andrea sat nearby, relishing the heat from a small coal fire. It was hot in the tent; she wore a blue work shirt and, as far as I could tell, nothing else.

When I opened my eyes and reminded myself that I was still alive, she smiled and wiped my face with a rag.

"Welcome to the world of the living," she said.

"I'm going back to sleep. Tell me we're really in a terrace apartment on Riverside Park."

She laughed. "We're about as far away from New York as you can get, but at least we're still alive."

I yawned and tried to push myself up to a sitting position. She pushed me back down against the ground.

"Stay still. Setka says you have a lot of resting to do. We'll be traveling soon."

"What do you mean?"

"Setka is going to dress us up as Mukhinos and take us across the Amur tomorrow at dawn," Andrea informed me.

"Why can't we go now?"

"Three reasons. I'm tired. You're wounded. And the Russians have trebled their patrol on the river."

"Good reasons," I said, feeling more tired by the second.

"Setka says that if you haven't made an overt attempt to cross the river by dawn, the Russians will assume you've headed in another direction and relax their guard."

"He must be right. My last two attempts to cross the river were disasters."

"Setka and his granddaughter are sleeping in another tent, so we have this to ourselves. He'll wake us an hour before dawn and rub some concoction on our faces and hands to make us look native. Then we'll ride to the Amur and cross as members of the tribe. Dawn will be a period of very low water, he says, and the Russian patrol boats won't be able to navigate."

"Setka is very good," I said. "I'll see if AXE can't put him on retainer."

"I think he'd probably be happiest just to see us gone," Andrea said.

"I don't know. He hates the Russians. In that regard, I seem to have brought a little light into his life."

Andrea nodded, and began fiddling with the top button of my shirt, fastening and unfastening it.

"Where do you suppose Rita is?" she asked.

"Back at camp, pretending to be worried sick about my disappearance and wondering what the hell happened to you. She may also have noticed a quantity of smoke from the direction of Trygda. If so, she will be one worried girl."

"What will you do with her?"

"I haven't made up my mind. There's a standard remedy, but I don't know if I'll apply it in her case. Let's get the hell out of Russia first."

Andrea had decided to leave my top button open, and was opening the rest. I sighed and closed my eyes while she pulled my shirt out of my pants and ran a hand over the muscles of my chest.

"I sent my two assistants to Tokyo to pick up some equipment," she said, rather distractedly. "For a few days at least, we're the only Americans here."

"Good," I replied.

Andrea unbuckled my belt, then turned suddenly and touched her fingertips to my cheek. "You've been hurt . . ." She hesitated, then continued softly, "I've wanted to make love to you from the moment we met. I denied it, because of the kind of work you do. Now, there's no point in denying anything. I . . ."

Sensing that her explanation would go on all night unless stopped, I put my hand over her mouth and said, "The time has come."

"Yes," she said, and quickly stripped off her blue shirt. I took her breasts and gently squeezed them, while her hands worked quickly to remove my pants.

The pigment on our faces and hands came from the fleshy leaves of a mountain weed. It stung my eyes until it was dry, and thereafter felt taut, like a mask. We were dressed in deerskins and cotton rags. Of our American provisions, all were gone save for weapons and my belt, which with its transmitter buckle, was hidden under the patched-up cotton shirt. If the Russians got close enough to me to conduct body searches, the game would be up anyway.

Andrea had to have her hair dyed and cut. That was the biggest problem. She gave every argument against cutting it. A reminder of what good her long hair would do her should the Russians catch us didn't suffice, at least not at first. In time, though, the deed was done, and by an hour before dawn, both Andrea and I looked as native as possible.

As the caravan drew up to the north bank of the Amur,

Andrea tightened her grip around my waist.

"Do you think we're going to make it?" she asked.

"We have to. You have your fossils to dig up, re-member?"

"That was so important to me, yet it seems so far away now."

"You'll get it back," I said.

"I hope so."

The river was in sight and we dismounted. There was a slight mist, a low-lying haze which rested atop the old river like a down blanket.

I walked to the edge and looked in both directions. If a patrol boat was nearby, there was no sign of it.

Setka came to me, looked around to assure himself of privacy and said, "Follow in line behind me. We will take a place in the middle of the line. The Russians know we are crossing this morning. I took great pains to tell one of their motorcycle officers, as I do each year. They will suspect nothing; but in any case, cannot get close to us with their boats."

"How deep will the water be?"

"Waist-high for you. More for the woman. How is your leg?"

"Better, thanks, and tightly bound. I will be able to walk."

"That is good. I want life to resume its old course. You must go home to America, and we must find the reindeer herds. They are most likely gone back south, into Chinese territory once again."

"Borders mean nothing to you, do they, old man?"

"Only what other men force upon us."

"How can you be sure the Russians won't inspect us as we cross the Amur?" I asked.

Setka laughed loudly and clapped me on the back. "The Russians think I speak only Mukhino, and maybe a dozen words in their dog's tongue, and that I am the most learned man in the tribe. They think us an amusement, not to be taken seriously. This time I think we prove them wrong, even if they can never know it."

"Your son and his woman . . . what of them?"

"I do not know. I like to think they will be let go one day. If not . . . maybe I will find a way to get them out."

"Maybe *I* will find a way to get them out."

"Perhaps. That is far in the future. Come . . . the tide is right, and it is time."

The Muhkinos were crossing the Amur, as they did twice every year, and with such regularity no one seemed to notice.

Andrea and I joined the line, bearing out packs—I carried the folded-up fabric of the tent under which we slept the night before. Andrea carried Setka's grandchild, who looked back at me, smiling with silent admiration.

Pack animals, dray horses and Indians walked solemnly through the water, across sand bars which lay near the surface at places known only to them. Andrea and I walked along, heads held high, balancing our loads and looking to the casual eye like regular tribe members.

I felt reasonably certain we blended in; a quarter mile to the upstream side, a Russian patrol boat identical to the one I sank held position against the current while two armed men watched us through binoculars.

They made no move toward us, nor showed any interest that was more than routine. It seemed too good to be true. After two failed attempts at fighting my way across the border, to just walk across seemed like an unreal dream.

When the entire tribe was across the river and safe on Chinese soil, Andrea and I put down our burdens and embraced.

Setka came to us, and said, "Our next camp is six miles to the south. We will be going now."

I shook his hand and, within a few minutes, the tribe had disappeared into the Manchurian woods.

"We're safe now," Andrea said.

"Let's get back to our camp and see how safe," I replied.

I took her hand and led her down a small deer trail which followed the south bank of the Amur.

TWENTY-SIX

The camp that the Chinese soldiers had hacked out of the woods near the site I had discovered had grown by the time Andrea and I got back to it. There was still no trail to it capable of supporting a vehicle. That was fine with me. I was sick to death of running away from motor patrols, and the sight of any kind of land vehicle put me off.

There were no new faces among the Chinese Army guards assigned to watch the expedition's equipment and work sight and do the manual labor. They were clustered about the cave entrance and spread around the nearby camp, resting from the effort of creating what they thought would be a long-term campsite. When Andrea and I walked up it was mid-afternoon. It had taken us the better part of the day to find our way back to the base, taking into consideration my leg wound and two rest stops.

The commander of the military forces on the scene (and Pao's second-in-command) was a Major Ti, a fat and loathsome career officer who I suspected of having little subtlety.

He knew why I was there; at least, he knew as much as Pao. When Andrea and I limped into the camp, exhausted and hungry as panthers, he came straight for me.

"There was smoke in the direction of Trygda. What happened?"

"Pao is dead. So is Trygda. Andrea and I are famished. We need something to eat."

"Did you get the lidanium?"

"No. But I avenged Pao's death. How about some food, major?"

"You are limping. Were you injured?"

"Yes. Shot in the thigh by a Russian colonel, who now lies dead, thanks to Andrea. How about some chow?"

"Chow?"

"Food. We'll take anything at this point."

"All right," Ti responded, somewhat irritably, motioning for us to approach our tents and at the same time waving at several functionaries who stood by the edge of the clearing.

"Oh, and one other thing . . ."

"What?" Ti said.

"Where's Rita?"

"The delightful Miss Brennan is in your tent, taking a nap. She reports not having slept well last night."

"I'm sure her nervous condition began when the smoke from Trygda was sighted."

"Now that you mention it, yes," Ti replied. "Is it important?"

"Nothing about Rita is important anymore. Come along, major, you'll want to hear this."

Andrea and the Chinaman followed me to the door of my tent, which was sealed against the afternoon sunlight.

"Call her, would you, major?"

Ti shrugged, and called Rita's name.

"What do you want?" was the sleepy reply.

"Come outside, please," he asked.

The canvas flap was pushed aside and Rita stepped into the

light, rubbing her eyes and looking like she had aged ten years overnight.

"Hello, Rita," I said.

She stopped. Perhaps her heart stopped; certainly her breath did. For several seconds she was paralyzed, then the surprise vanished and she made a fast move for a slender knife she had tucked under her belt.

My right fist arched out and caught the point of her chin, throwing Rita backward into my tent, which collapsed under her weight. The knife skidded a few yards away. Andrea picked it up.

"I don't understand," Major Ti said.

"Rita is a Russian agent. She's responsible for Pao's death and the Russians finding out about the mission."

Ti barked an order and two Chinese soldiers ran over, guns at the ready. They pulled Rita to her feet. We watched as her hands were bound; she was defiant, and flashed me an evil look.

The Chinese soldiers led her off. I turned to the major. "She's your prisoner," I said. "I don't want anything more to do with her."

"I have a feeling Peking will find something to do with her," he said. "I will see to your food, and have your tent put back up."

Andrea and I changed our clothes. I replaced my bandage with something a bit less informal, and gave myself a shot of American penicillin to be sure. While the food was being dished out, I saw the Chinese major on the far side of the camp, conferring with aides and gesturing wildly with his hands.

Ti came to my tent when we were nearly done eating and stood looking down at us as we scraped the plates clean.

"Peking will have to be told that you did not get the lidanium," he said.

"I guess so," I replied.

"Peking will not be happy."

"Neither will Washington. And frankly, major, I'm not too pleased myself."

"This whole thing is preposterous. May I sit down?" Ti joined us on the ground, but not without some difficulty and only after carefully arranging a bed of clean pine needles to prevent Manchurian soil from touching his uniform pants. "How was the food? No, don't tell me. This isn't Peking. You can't like it any better than I do."

"I don't."

"Very well then, tell me what happened while you were on Russian soil."

I told him, leaving out the part about finding the lidanium and disposing of it later on in the Amur. Andrea listened quietly, registering no emotion as I spun my tale of explosions and death.

When I was done, he asked, "What about the lidanium. There was no trace of it?"

"A slight register on my counter."

"But no metal?"

"Nothing I could gather up and haul away. The counter gave a general indication for an area several yards square. My guess is that the lidanium was dispersed by the force of the impact. I did not have time to pick it all up."

"That, at least, is understandable," Ti said. "If nothing else, you seem to have punished the Russians for building fortifications close to our border."

The point wasn't worth arguing. Let the Russians argue for themselves. "Sure," I said.

"If as you say the metal is not retrievable," he went on, "the mission is ended, and I assume you will be taking the first plane back to the West."

"No," Andrea said, and I nodded.

"What?" the major asked, surprised.

"We have on our hands an important archaeological find," she said. "It cannot be simply ignored. There is work to be done."

"But the Russians . . ."

"Will launch a retalliatory strike," I finished the sentence for him. "But against a Chinese settlement, not a wilderness area. If I were you, I would look to fortifying Aihui."

Ti looked shocked and I honestly believe the thought never occurred to him. No wonder he was serving in wildest Manchuria.

"They may not attack us," he said, cautiously.

"Of course they will. A Chinese intelligence agent's body lies on their soil, as do several Chinese weapons. The Russians have all the excuse they need to blow the hell out of Aihui or some other border town."

Ti got to his feet, and a bit faster than he sat down. "I must consult Peking on this. I will inform you of what is decided. You will *not* be leaving camp, then?"

"I may leave *camp*. I might take a swim, go fishing, or just wander into the woods. But Andrea will be working in the cave for at least another week, and I will not leave her."

"Very well," the major said, and hurried off.

"Take a swim?" Andrea asked.

"Tonight, around midnight."

"The stream's too shallow," she protested.

"The Amur will do nicely," I replied.

"I think you're out of your mind," Andrea said.

"What have you got against swimming?" I asked, sitting on a tuft of grass which rose like a footstool from the soft, mossy bank.

We were on a low, flat patch of riverbank protected by overhanging spruce branches. As I stripped off my clothes, I could see the very top corner of the cabin of the patrol boat I sank breaking the surface of the river.

"Nothing, under normal circumstances. But the Russians are nearby, I suppose, and they're *mad* at us, Nick."

"Yeah, but they won't send any boats over here."

"Why not?"

"There's a sunken obstruction."

"How do you know?"

"I sank it myself," I said, with some pride.

"Even so . . . I bet it's cold in that water."

"Nope. I was in it twice already today, and it isn't bad at all. You waded in it, for God's sake."

"It was *cold*."

"Once you're submerged you won't even notice," I said.

"Nick, first you make an ostentatious display of disappearing into the woods with a bottle of booze, and me. Now you don't want to eat or drink—you want to swim. What the hell is up?"

"That was really done to make our Chinese friends think that we were only going out to engage in a little Western decadence. Actually, I have some work to do. You can stay on shore if you like, but it would help if the Chinese see you come back to camp wet."

Andrea sighed and unbuckled her belt. "The things I do for America," she mumbled.

I dove into the water which, was a little brisker than I had remembered. A moon was shinging through a gauze of cirrus clouds. There was a light down the river which I took to be the running light of a Russian patrol boat. Whatever it was, the light was too far away to represent danger.

There was a splash, and I was joined in the water. Andrea came up behind me, put her arms around me and gave me a hug.

"It's not so bad," she said.

I spun and faced her, pulled her to me and felt her breast press against my chest.

Then I turned and dived beneath the water and swam along the bottom to where I had jettisoned the lidanium. It took four dives to find it, but find it I did. I swam back to Andrea with the sack I had made with my wool socks and displayed it as proudly as a housecat showing off a slaughtered mouse.

"Got it."

"What's that?"

"The lidanium. What else?"

"But you said you never found it," she protested.

"I lied," I said, slipping my arms around her and pulling her underwater.

TWENTY-SEVEN

"What was to be gained by lying to the Chinese about the lidanium?" Andrea asked, after we came up for air.

"What damage was done? I bought myself some time to figure out if they're honest or not."

"And if the Chinese seem to be honest?"

"I'll share the loot with them, of course. But not here, where it's too easy for accidents to happen. In Tientsin or Shanghai, where the transaction can be seen by friendly eyes."

"You could have shared the secret with me," she said, a bit ruefully.

"Not while there was still danger of capture by the Russians. Had that happened, you'd be better off not knowing."

Andrea nodded, pushed away from me and dived. I swam to the shore, got out and hid the lidanium next to the hassock of grass I sat on while taking off my clothes. I dived back in the water and swam to Andrea, and for twenty minutes we splashed around as if we hadn't a care in the world. She

169

seemed to be forcing herself to play in order not to think of something, and before long I found out what it was.

Lying in the sandy shallows holding hands, our heads on the low, mossy bank, Andrea asked, "What happens if the Chinese *aren't* being honest?"

"They'll try to kill us and take *all* the lidanium for themselves. We'll have to do the best we can."

"Oh. More bloodshed, I suppose."

"Maybe the Chinese are being straight with us. I could get lucky. It's about time."

"Well," she said, philosophically, "I suppose if I *have* to abandon the dig, all won't be lost. I got some wonderful stuff out already—enough to fit into a small bag. And there are pictures of everything, thanks to Rita."

I chuckled at the mention of her name.

"What will they do to her?" Andrea asked.

"They could be stupid and shoot her or put her on trial. Or they could be smart and trade her to the Russians for Pao's body and the agreement to keep yesterday's activities quiet. Who the hell knows?"

"Don't you care?"

"Andrea, the lady sold me out and left me to be killed. Am I supposed to feel sorry for her?"

"I just thought . . ."

"A random guess is that Rita will be roughed up a little and then traded with Moscow. She'll probably turn up back in Western Europe in a few years. These people have a way of reinfecting my life. I expect I haven't seen the last of her."

Back in something resembling western beds at last, Andrea and I slept almost to noon. We bathed in the stream. I shaved using a mirror propped up on a stream-side boulder, and went off to the cave to carry on the excavation. I wanted her to get as much out as she could in case a hasty departure was called for.

In keeping with the old theory that the best place to hide a tree is in a forest, I took the lidanium from its pouch and tossed it into Andrea's sample bag along with the several dozen flints she collected. And the radiation wouldn't do us much harm in the short periods of time the bag would be in our company.

With nothing better to do than watch the Chinese Army soldiers play backgammon and brag of their exploits with women back in Peking, I amused myself by conning weapons out of my guests. The technique was simplicity itself. All I did was insult the quality of the home-grown armor until a sample was given to me to test. I wound up with a type 51 Tokarev, a box of ammunition and enough paper targets to try it out with.

I went a quarter mile into the woods and fired a dozen rounds with the automatic pistol, the capabilities of which I already knew well enough. I wanted my friends back at camp to think I had been really practicing. That done, I sat leaning against a tree and prepared to spend the day waiting for the other shoe to fall. I had already heard from the Russians; now I would learn what the Chinese move would be. Major Ti would certainly be hearing from Peking before long.

The other shoe fell before I was seated even for a half an hour.

I saw a jeep coming up the newly-cut trail from the patrol road. In it was Arthur Pendle. He never went into the field, and I assumed his arrival was bad news. I went to meet him, sticking the Tokarev into my belt as if it were my own.

Ti reached the vehicle at the same time as me, "Who are you?" he asked.

"Arthur Pendle, Propylon Trading Company."

"Trading Company?" Ti repeated suspiciously.

"Shanghai, Tientsin and Hong Kong," Pendle said, pumping the major's hand effusively. "I arranged the scientific expedition's tour." He turned to me and said "Professor Rainsford! How good to see you again."

"The same," I replied.

"I brought your camera. The Nikon people finally have

the shutter working properly, or so they say. Here you are.''

"He placed a brand-new 35mm camera in my hands. I improvised: "Thanks, Pendle. The microphotography will be a lot simpler now."

"Do you know this man?" Ti asked me.

"Of course. He arranged the expedition's travel arrangement, as he said. I didn't expect him quite so soon with the Nikon, though."

"We aim to please," Pendle said. "But I'm afraid I can't be so obliging as regards to your two researchers who are in Tokyo. There were unforeseen problems with the equipment. They shan't be back for a week at the least."

"Damn," I said.

"Yes, I know. Dr. Regan will be disappointed. Is she around?"

"At the site. Want to see it? Do you mind, major?"

Ti shrugged and wandered off. I led Pendle up the footpath leading to the cave, and as soon as we were out of earshot of the Chinese, I remarked, "The shit hit the fan, huh?"

"Not yet, but it's threatening to do so."

"I knew you wouldn't leave your office unless there was a good reason."

"Right. I have it on very good authority that the Chinese have decided to kill you and take the lidanium all for themselves. I don't know if the order has reached Major Ti."

"I'm still alive, if that's any indication. No, I don't think Ti has the order yet. A complicating factor is they think I didn't get the goods."

"Do they? You got it, of course."

"It's in my tent. About twenty pounds, and it looks like pretty good stuff to me."

"If the Chinese think you didn't get it, there's a chance you can get out of the country. Of course, you'll be searched, and I would think rather carefully. No, I don't suppose you would get out of the country in that case."

"I have to leave before Ti gets the orders to shoot me," I said.

"If you can convince him you still have a shot at finding the lidanium . . . no, I don't suppose that would work, either. You'll have to leave immediately. *We'll* have to leave. My God, what the hell am I doing in the field? I had really figured on dying in bed."

"Sorry, Pendle."

"Oh, who cares? You did some job the other day, might I add. The military grapevine was buzzing with it. The Russians are preparing to claim the Chinese launched a provocative raid on one of their border outposts."

"The Russians and I disagreed," I said. "And I won the argument."

I filled Pendle in on the details of my hours on Siberian soil. He nodded solemnly, now and then showing a glimmering of excitement and approval. I sensed he really did want to be in the field, no matter what he said. He was sure in it now.

"So it *was* Rita," he said when I was done.

"Yeah."

"Did you take care of the problem?"

"I gave her to the Chinese. Ti has her someplace, or maybe he sent her to Peking."

"They'll no doubt try to trade her off to Moscow in return for peace on the border." Pendle suggested.

"That was my thought."

"I wish I could listen to the diplomatic signals. They're sure to be priceless. No matter. We'll have to use the Beagle to get out. She's still at Aihui, with a full tank and only one guard."

"Aihui *is* a distance away, and has a radio," I said.

"Aihui *is* a distance away, but it no longer has a radio. At least, it no longer has one that is operable. My pilot had the lack of sense to leave me alone for two minutes in order to relieve his bladder. Unless Aihui is spectaculary well-equipped with spare parts, it has no radio until a hand-carried message can make it, on the regular flights, to Harbin and back. That would be the day after tomorrow at the earliest."

"Nice job, Pendle. Now if you can just knock out the radio

in Major Ti's jeep, we'll be all set."

He shrugged. "So what if he can contact Peking? He cannot contact Aihui, and that is where the aerocraft sits."

"If we get to this aerocraft," I said, imitating Pendle's accent, "where the hell are we supposed to go in it? We're in the middle of Manchuria."

"Where else? The corridor where Vladivostock is to be found; the Chinese, Russian and Korean borders join there, right at the sea. There is hope that some judicious low-level flying will get us far out into the Sea of Japan before our absence is noticed. I have asked your Pacific fleet to keep an ear out for a distress signal. They're on maneuvers in the Sea of Japan. Did I tell you?"

"I heard something about it," I replied.

"I understand you fly?"

"I dabble," I said.

"Well, then, let's find Dr. Regan and tell her that, the pressures of archaeology notwithstanding, you're going to dabble in flying within the next few hours."

TWENTY-EIGHT

"It's a shame to leave this all behind," Andrea said, packing the last of her tiny picks into a canvas case.

The Chinese version of a Coleman lamp cast knife-sharp shadows around the inside of the cave. We were alone, Pendle having stayed in camp to see if he could scrounge up some stuff for me.

"You got enough to keep you busy for five years," I said.

"Three, maybe four years."

"And with your reputation now enhanced, you won't have any trouble getting grants. Don't complain to me. I think I set you up for life. At any rate, escaping with three or four years work is preferable to what the Chinese have in mind for us."

"It's hard to believe they really mean to kill us."

"They want the lidanium, and maybe they don't believe I didn't get it. They might mistrust me."

"Oh, I can't imagine *that*," she said sarcastically.

"And when the Russians attack Aihui, Peking might want something to give them other than Rita. I'm valuable to

Moscow. They've been dying to get their hands on me for years.''

"Considering Trygda, I suppose that's literally true.''

"It is.''

"What if they *don't* attack Aihui?'' she asked.

"They will.''

"You don't *know* that.''

"Sure I do,'' I insisted.

"Why? It's been forty-eight hours and they haven't yet.''

"Trust me.''

"No way. Why should I be any better than the Chinese? Come on, help me get this junk out of here.''

We left the lamp burning alone in the cave, and carried out two canvas duffels packed with samples, charts, drawings and tools. They weighed a hundred pounds, and taken with the bag Andrea kept in her tent, made quite a load. The road to the airfield was a long one, and I would have to have a jeep anyway. I tossed the duffels into the back of the jeep used to transport the heavier equipment to and from the cave. Andrea climbed into the back and I slid alongside the driver.

"To the camp.'' I said.

The vehicle rolled easily onto the newly-cut trail leading down the hill from the cave, through a short stand of spruce, and to the camp. I took the two bags into my tent and lay them next to Andrea's other one, taking a few seconds to assure myself that that the lidanium was where I left it.

Andrea had gone off someplace, but Pendle came up, took me aside and said, "I got what you wanted. It's wrapped in a tarp under your cot.''

"A mortar? They actually have mortars here?''

"No. But I got a Goryunov grenade launcher with a dozen rounds. It cost me only a hundred pounds. The corporal who arranged to lose it in the woods thinks he suckered me. I neglected to tell him a piece like that is worth two thousand dollars American any day of the week.''

"Did you have to explain to this corporal what you wanted it for?''

"Of course. He is curious, if not overly astute at business. I told him I run a thriving smuggling operation in Chinese arms, which are prized throughout the western world for their quality."

"And he swallowed it?"

"He took the hundred pounds. Actually, I have done a bit of gun-running, just to keep the alibi active. The Chinese admire under-the-counter enterprises, as long as they get something out of it, in this case a few pounds and flattery."

"I'm grateful, Pendle."

"To satisfy *my* curiosity. What *do* you want the grenade launcher for? I hope you're not planning on going out and getting yourself killed in the next few hours. I was planning to fly out of here soon, and you're the only qualified pilot among the three of us."

"The other day I lit a fuse which is taking entirely too long to burn," I said. "I'm going to go out this evening and shorten it."

"You're *not*." Pendle said with a mixture of fear and glee.

"I sure as hell am," I replied.

The fires were out in Trygda, but even at midnight the outpost glowed as brightly as when the flames were their highest.

Lights were set up everywhere, and two large patrol boats continuously swept both Russian and Chinese banks with powerful searchlights.

I crept the last hundred yards on my belly, avoiding the spotlights by flattening myself against the ground when they approached. The grenade launcher was strapped to my back, and once again my pockets were crammed with explosives.

On the two-hour hike to that piece of border, I passed three Chinese patrols on two separate military roads. Perhaps spurred by my warning about Aihui, the Chinese were pouring troops into the area. The Russians had done the same thing, prompted by the fires of Trygda. The situation was the powder keg of legend.

I really wasn't out to create an international incident. I just wanted Ti and his men to have something more pressing than me on their minds. But if to do so required the creation of an international incident, I was better prepared than anyone to do it.

The new patrol boats, brought up the Amur at considerable trouble and expense, were twice the size of the old. They were flat-bottomed, shallow-draft vessels with 50mm cannons mounted fore and aft, capable of carrying several dozen troops. The searchlights were mounted atop the cabin roof and easy targets. I didn't want them. They were contributing to the general commotion, and commotion was what I meant to encourage.

On the Russian bank I saw hundreds of men. Some were pulling apart the charred bones of the ruined buildings; others lounging with their platoons awaiting orders. Further away from the water I saw the outlines of two amphibious personnel carriers. So the Russians *were* planning a counter-attack after all. But by the bored look of their troops, it didn't figure to be soon. That is, not unless I shortened the fuse.

This was going to be as dangerous a strike as I ever attempted. I would have less than thirty seconds to fire all twelve grenades. That done, I would have to run like hell for a mile or more, then jog the rest of the way back to camp.

The Russians would take just about half a minute to start pouring ordnance into my side of the river bank. They would most likely give the whole bank a good pasting, then load their troops aboard the personnel carriers for a trip the few miles up the river to Aihui. They should attack the Chinese town, I figured, just about as I was getting back to camp. With any luck, the timing would be perfect.

I fitted a grenade onto the muzzle of the launcher and figured the distance. I took some time estimating the angle, wind and distance. Economy of fire was called for, and also I had to be certain not to damage the personnel carriers. This was to be a provocation, and no more. I had shed enough

Russian blood already. A few well-placed shots in the trees along the periphery of the outpost should piss them off enough to take action.

A tall, thin man in the uniform of a lieutenant general walked slowly by the river bank, his hands clasped behind his back. I started firing.

Three were in the air before the first one landed, impacting in the woods to the northwest of the river piers. The lieutenant general unclasped his hands and hit the dirt as his troops were roused from their lethargy and did likewise.

My dozen grenades exploded around the perimeter of the base, the last two landing in the center of the clearing, representing the final insult. I abandoned my Chinese weapon and ran.

Within seconds, small arms fire erupted from the Russian bank. Not much later, Russian mortars and tactical rockets filled my side of the river with flame. It hadn't rained in more than two weeks; the fire was sure to be impressive. I kept to the main trail, running at a marathoner's pace until the first mile was done, then slowing to a medium jog.

I estimated a twenty-minute run back to camp. The Russians stopped firing after five of those minutes, and I could envision them piling into their amphibious personnel carriers for the retalliatory assault on Aihui.

I stopped jogging a quarter-mile outside the camp, and sat by the base of a short, fat spruce beneath which I had hidden a half-empty bottle of scotch. I caught my breath, took several swigs and stumbled back into camp. Major Ti was on me in a flash. "Where were you?" he asked.

"Where does it look like?" I replied, offering him the bottle.

"No, thank you. Have you nothing better to do than roam the woods getting drunk?"

"No," I said. "I found the damn cave for Andrea, quite by accident I admit. But if you think I'm going to crawl around on my hands and knees sifting through bones for her, you're out of your mind. She's well equipped to do it on her own, and, if not, her assistants will return from Tokyo in a few days. What's on your mind, Ti?''

"I heard what sounded like gunfire.''

I shrugged. "Nothing near me, I assure you. I couldn't hit the broad side of a barn in the shape I'm in.''

A vague smile touched his lips, and he smiled. For a second I almost liked him. "You will have trouble with your government, won't you? About the lidanium?''

"I'll make a deal with you,'' I replied. "I won't try to predict the reaction of my government if you don't try to tell me what Peking is up to. We're fighting men, Ti, not damn politicians.''

The major liked the compliment, and seemed about to say something, but he was interrupted.

A functionary appeared from the direction of the truck used as command center for radio communications. He stammered, "Russian attack on Aihui, sir! Two invasion boats filled with men! We have been ordered to the scene!''

"Oh, shit,'' I said, in feigned drunkenness, "I wonder what the hell Peking is going to say about that.''

Major Ti looked around him in apparent confusion for a time, then turned his attention back to me. "You will stay here, and your party with you. Three men will be assigned to see that you do. I am sorry, but I simply do not trust you. When my men and I have dealt with the Russian threat, we will be back and resume the discussion.''

"Don't wake me up,'' I said, taking a swig of scotch to accent the point.

TWENTY-NINE

I watched as three Chinese guards ran over to where I was standing and placed themselves around me, as if to suggest that I needed to be surrounded to be watched safely.

Major Ti walked stiffly to his jeep, barking orders at his driver. The hapless corporal was switching the ignition on and off, mouthing silent curses at a machine which refused to operate. Ti yelled at the driver, and at the jeep, finally kicking it in the side and stalking off. The driver trailed after, and as I smiled at the sight, the Chinese guards pushed me across the camp and into my tent.

Pendle and Andrea sat on the floor cross-legged, playing cards and drinking tea.

"Do the guards speak English?" I asked.

"Not a word," Pendle replied, without looking up.

"Then we're safe to talk. The Russians have attacked Aihui."

Pendle looked up, and he smiled viciously. "What a bloody shame. I suppose Major Ti will have to rush to reinforce the garrison."

"He just left. Had some problem with his jeep and had to leave it behind, though."

From his shirt pocket, Pendle produced a small steel band that was but slightly stained with lubricating oil. "They always work better with the rotor in," he said, tossing it to me.

I nodded appreciatively and stuck the rotor in a pants pocket.

"The Russian outpost at Trygda suffered another assault," I reported. "They had moved in several dozen troops, and two amphibious carriers. A lieutenant general was in charge."

"A general? So they *are* taking the matter seriously, after all. I only hope that in punishing Aihui they neglect the airfield."

"It's a good distance inland from the town, and when I was on Russian soil I saw nothing that poses a serious threat of strafing."

"I'm rather inclined to believe they wouldn't call in air support if they could," Pendle said. "Air support makes their punishment of Aihui an act far in excess of what it's designed to punish. No, they will do the equivalent of what they think the Chinese did—send in a few dozen men to burn the town."

Pendle threw down his cards, got to his feet and said, "Dr. Regan plays a mean game of poker."

"She does a lot of things well," I replied.

Andrea stood and came to me. I held her for a moment. Her silence when I entered the tent could only be taken for fear of death mixed with resignation to the inevitable. "Are we going now?" she asked, her voice breaking.

"As soon as we fix the guards."

"What do you want me to do?"

"Is everything packed and ready to go?"

She nodded.

"Then sit on the cot. This won't take long."

Andrea did as she was told, but her shoulders sagged and she hid her face in her hands.

"Where are the guards?" Pendle asked.

"Two in front, one in the back. They think I'm drunk."

"You *do* look rather like someone who's about to become ill. Outside with you . . . can't have accidents on Uncle Sam's property."

Still holding the bottle of scotch, I began coughing and endured several seconds of Pendle chewing me out loudly in English. At last, Pendle put an arm around my shoulders and led me out the door, yelling in Mandarin, "This fool is drunk! He's going to vomit in the tent!"

With disgusted glances, the two guards out front slung their weapons across their shoulders and came to my aid, while the third walked curiously around from behind the tent.

It was ridiculously simple. I bent low and pretended to retch then stumble and fall, until one of the Chinese rushed in and took me roughly by the back of my shirt. I brought my head up sharply, catching him on the chin and driving his lower jaw into the roof of his mouth. I heard the crunch of teeth breaking off at the roots and a gasping cry.

Pendle dropped his companion with a right to the stomach and a left to the head. For a desk jockey, he was pretty good.

I spun toward the third man and hurled the half-empty bottle of scotch at his head. I missed, but the Chinese was thrown off balance. He fell onto his side, the machine gun trapped beneath him. As he struggled to get it out, I raced the ten yards and leaped onto him, driving my stiletto into his heart.

The whole thing was over in a few seconds, and not a shot was fired. By the time I got back to the front of the tent, Pendle had relieved the two bodies there of their weapons and ammunition.

"You should have been a field operative, Pendle. You've missed your calling sitting at that desk in Shanghai."

He looked quite pleased with himself.

"If you'll give me back that rotor," he said, "I'll see to the transportation."

I gave him the strip of metal, and went in to Andrea. She was roused out of her torpor; she had the three large bags ready by the door.

"That was quick," she said.

"There were only three of them."

"I seem to be getting used to this. Are we ready to go?"

I picked up two of the bags and led her out to the jeep. There was no sign of life around the camp. Major Ti had, in fact, taken all but three of his men to fight the Russians at Aihui. Pendle had the hood up on the Chinese jeep and was repairing the distributor, using the light from a pocket flashlight. I tossed the bags into the back of the jeep.

"Done," Pendle said, and slammed the hood shut.

I heard a noise then, a muffled wail in response to the slamming of the hood. The sound came from Ti's command tent, a green-yellow tent twice the size called for by the dimensions of the camp.

"What was that?" Andrea asked.

"If I'm not mistaken," I replied, "it's more baggage."

Pendle grinned, got behind the wheel of the jeep and kicked over the engine. I walked quickly to the tent, threw open the flaps and stepped inside. Rita was sitting on the dirt floor, tied to the center post, a gag over her mouth. I knelt in front of her, and couldn't help but grin. I pulled down the gag.

"Paul . . . thank God it's you!"

I shook my head. "Stop it, Rita, and make up your mind . . . do you want to stay here or come back to America with me?"

"I—uh—I—"

"I'm leaving," I said, and started to go.

"No! Take me! The Chinese are barbarians. I know I won't be tortured in America."

I put the gag back around her mouth, freed her from the

pole, but left her hands tied. I carried her to the jeep and tossed her in the back along with the bags of Andrea's samples.

Andrea glared at Rita in shameless triumph, then looked away. I climbed into the vehicle and we were off.

Pendle took the trail which led in the direction of Shun-wu before hooking up with a secondary road into Aihui. The road straight into Aihui was the route Ti and his men followed, and close to the Amur. The last thing I wanted was to run into them or, worse, any Russians who might be looking for them.

The Shun-wu road had the advantage of curving far from the river. It was only two miles longer, and did join with a major military road. But there would likely be no traffic that time of night, and since Pendle knocked out the Aihui transmitter, no calls for help to the base outside Harbin, the capital of Manchuria.

Pendle drove rapidly down the crude dirt roads, stopping every so often to shut off the engine and listen for the sounds of battle. The first two stops we heard nothing. But the third and final stop was only a mile south of the airfield; from it the sound of sporadic gunfire could be made out.

"How far away, do you think?" Pendle asked.

"At least two miles."

"The fighting would be in town, then," he said. "I guess we'll be safe."

"Where is the plane tied down?"

"By the far end of the field, I'm sorry to say."

"Okay, let's go. But very slowly and with the lights out."

Pendle started up the engine one last time, put the transmission in gear and let up on the clutch. We moved slowly down the road.

THIRTY

The B.206 Beagle was parked near the end of the runway closest to the village of Aihui, Manila lines holding her wheels fast to wooden pegs set in the ground.

We drove straight down the landing strip, lights out, with me standing up holding one of the Chinese machine guns we acquired at the camp. There was the glow of fire in the direction of the village; now and again a slender flame reached above the treetops. By the time we reached the plane, the gunfire was audible above the engine of the jeep.

"Jesus," Andrea whispered as the engine shut down.

"Yeah. Let's get the bags aboard. Pendle, can you hot-wire that thing?"

"I'll have a go at it," he said, and went to apply his talent for tampering with electronic gadgets to the control console of the twin-engine plane. I lowered the bags to the ground and carried them to the plane. The passenger door was unlocked easily enough, and the three bags of Andrea's tools and samples tucked into the last three of the eight seats in the aircraft. I carried Rita—still gagged and bound—to a fourth seat and buckled her in. She squirmed and indicated for me to remove the gag, but it stayed on.

"Typical British ingenuity on this ignition," Pendle called. "Simple and to the point; only two wires. It's fixed now—fire the engine-starts and she's ready."

The sound of gunfire grew nearer and the flames bright enough to illuminate the forest backdrop. The tall, slender trunks of the pitch pines stood like matchsticks against the light of exploding incendiaries. Now and then, I could see a figure moving from trunk to trunk, retreating in our direction.

"The good major seems to be taking a pasting," Pendle called out.

"No kidding. Come on, let's cut the ropes and get the hell out of here."

"What do you want me to do?" Andrea asked.

"Have a seat and keep your head down," I replied.

I hopped out of the plane, ran round to the starboard side (the side nearest Aihui) and used my stiletto to cut the quarter-inch line holding the starboard landing gear to the ground. Pendle did the same for the port side.

A shot came very nearby, then a whistling and the impact of a long-range grenade splintered a batch of scrub oak not far from the operations shack. "Fire her up, Pendle!" I yelled.

There was a hush, and a figure coming out of the woods to the edge of the field. It was Major Ti, not arrogant this time but dirty, sweat-soaked and scared. With him were three soldiers—the vanguard of the retreating Chinese troops. Badly outmanned and out-gunned, they had the same idea as me—grab the airplane and get the hell out.

Ti spotted me and, for a pregnant half-second, was frozen in surprise and indecision. Then I saw his jaw harden and the tip of the machine gun in his hand come up.

I was faster than him. I poured half a magazine into his bulging gut, ripping it open and spilling his insides across the beaten-down grass on the edge of the airfield. The men with him were stunned only a second before they returned fire.

I hit the dirt and, at the same time, heard the Beagle's twin engines kick into life. Bullets kicked up the turf beneath me and slammed into the fuselage of the airplane above.

Two Russian grenades tore up the grass a hundred yards away, and for a second the Chinese guns stopped. I jumped up, emptied my gun in the direction of the woods, then dropped it and dived under the fuselage. I came up on the port side, ripped open the door and dived into the plane.

In the dim light I saw Andrea hunched over, keeping down as she was told. I hurried into the pilot's seat, pushed the throttles forward, and the Beagle rolled across the grass toward the north end of the runway.

Pendle was pressed against the starboard window, beyond which the entire northern forest seemed to be ablaze with the border conflict I had begun. The smell of smoke came through the holes in the fuselage. I turned the small craft onto the runway and opened up the throttles. Several more holes appeared as the Beagle gained speed, its headlamps picking out a straight path down the dirt track. At sixty the plane felt light; at seventy-two I eased back on the control column and the nose came up. We were airborne. As we rose above the tree tops, a great feeling of lightness came over me. We were neither on Russian nor Chinese soil; we were flying.

I clapped Pendle on the back, and said, "We did it! We're up!"

Pendle reacted to my touch by falling off his seat and into the aisle. His eyes were wide open, his chest ripped apart by a slug. He was dead. Andrea screamed and looked away.

"Drag him back," I said.

"My God! No!"

"He's in the way. His feet are in the way of the rudders. Pull him back near Rita."

"Nick! Please!"

"If you want to fly the plane, I'll do it."

She thought a second, then took Pendle by the arms and pulled him out of the way and down the aisle to the aft section of the plane.

"Come up here," I said.

She slipped into Pendle's co-pilot's seat and immediately grabbed hold of my arm. "Why did he have to die? He was such a nice man."

"Why? Because that's what happens when you're out in the field."

"He was *your friend*. How can you be so callous?"

"Pendle was an associate, not my friend. I barely knew the man. He, however, knew exactly what he was getting into. When he flew to Aihui, Pendle knew he wasn't coming out. He died nobly, and was proud of himself."

Andrea shook her head, not comprehending but at least not arguing with me.

"Can you read a map?" I asked.

"Yes . . . sure," she said, pulling herself out of it.

"I'll need your help. There are sure to be maps here someplace. Try in that compartment to the right of the co-pilot's steering column. There should be a reading lamp around, too."

"Where are we going?"

"To the sea. We'll be flying south-southeast, following the Amur for a time, then cutting across the Ho-chiang bulge to cross the junction of the Chinese, North Korean and Russian borders near Vladivostok. I have a pretty good idea of the route, but we have to watch for mountains?"

"Mountains?"

"We'll be flying at five hundred feet or less," I explained. "Unbuckle my belt and take it off."

Andrea looked confused, but did as I asked. She held the buckle up to the light long enough for me to find the contact points and press them in sequence.

"What does that do?" she asked.

"Send out an automated distress signal and homing beacon to United States naval forces on maneuvers in the Sea of Japan. We may need their assistance, once we get the hell off this continent."

"How long will that take?"

"A little under three hours."

Andrea rummaged for maps and before long found an up-to-date aeronautical chart of the Manchurian region. There were few population centers and only three airfields all the way from Aihui on a straight line to the Vladivostok corridor. My first job would be to get over the Lesser Khingans. As most of the peaks were under three thousand feet, it would be no problem.

"I'm going to take us up to five thousand until we're over the mountains."

"Won't we show up on radar screens?"

"Sure, but there shouldn't be any around. The chart doesn't show any installations between here and Chi-hsi. There are civilian fields at that town and at Mu-tan-chiang to the southwest. They might have radar. But they're pretty near the coast and on flat terrain. It will be near daylight by the time we get there. I can safely drop down to tree-top level and fly under the radar."

"If you say so."

I pulled back on the wheel and inched the throttles forward. Within minutes we were at three thousand five hundred and slipping over a series of small, rounded peaks west of the tiny village of K'u-ssu-t e. Beyond a similar ridge which lay parallel and ten miles in front was a large basin occupied by nothing more dangerous than reindeer. At five thousand feet I leveled off and flicked on the autopilot.

Andrea wanted to be held, and that is just what I did, stroking her hair and letting her gain strength by resting a cheek on my shoulder.

After a time, I said, "I'm sorry about Pendle, I really am. He was a good man. I wish I had gotten to know him better. Let me look at him."

I straightened up the body and pulled it to the very back of the cabin. In his wallet was the usual array of false documents, two hundred and some-odd pounds, and a much handled color photo of a middle-aged couple standing with three young children. The woman had the same features as Pendle, and was no doubt his sister. I would have to write her.

Rita was complaining again and struggling against her bonds. I brought her up to the seat behind the co-pilot's, where Andrea sat staring blankly out the windshield. I strapped her in, then retied her hands so they were more comfortably in front of her. I pulled down the gag.

"If you've got something to say, make it good."

"You don't expect to pull this off, do you?" she said.

"Pull what off?" I asked, slipping back into the pilot's seat and checking the fuel gauge. It showed enough fuel to take us out of Manchuria and over international waters, but just barely.

"Getting out of this alive."

"I've done pretty good so far. No thanks to you. Hey, if you don't have anything worthwhile to tell me, I'm going to put the gag back on."

"I want to talk."

"Talk."

"Not in front of her."

"Andrea isn't listening to you. I doubt she ever did. *Talk.*"

"There's no need to get us all killed running away," Rita said.

"Isn't there?"

"No. We could land at Vladivostok. You'll be well-treated. Her too."

"Is that all you have to offer? Surrender?"

"It's better than dying."

"Not in my book, lady. Tell me something more interesting."

"You're not going to bend, are you? No, I don't suppose you are." She laughed bitterly. "So then we'll die. My people will shoot us down."

"I doubt it," I replied.

"Russian planes are very efficient."

"Sure, and also unaware of my presence. You forget that you're the only one to get out of Trygda with knowledge of my existence, and you thought I was a goner. No, if the Russian air force is sending up planes, I would think they'd send them to Trygda or Aihui. And even if they do catch word of our escape attempt, they'll have to enter Chinese airspace to get me."

"Not when you fly over the Vladivostok corridor."

"I admit that one will be tricky. I'm counting on getting lost in the general confusion."

"What confusion?" she asked.

"The confusion that will result when the air forces of three nations converge to shoot us down," I said.

Andrea looked at me then. "Is *that* what you're counting on?" She gulped.

"It's all the chance we have."

THIRTY-ONE

Two railroad tracks ran parallel and about thirty miles apart southwest of Chi-hsi. They were the last such lines before I would see the track from Pos'yet to Vladivostok and my last glimpse of the Asian continent, I was back down at five hundred feet, at times lower, and yet had seen no sign of life on the ground.

The radio was a different story. The Chinese military frequency used by their fighter base at Harbin was very much alive. They got word of my three-hour flight to freedom an hour before it was to end, and wasted half that time looking for me in the wrong places. For some reason—perhaps relating to Rita's having disappeared at the same time—the commander of the Harbin base got the notion we were heading for the Russian base at Khabarovsk, near the extreme northeast corner of Manchuria.

A squadron of MIG-21's was sent in pursuit, and crossed our trail heading northeast as we were flying southeast and far in the distance. By the time the squadron was recalled, we were flying over an uninhabited woodland coming up fast on the junction of the three borders. They could catch us, as could the second squadron dispatched from the Chinese base at Mukden, but only at the peril of entering Soviet or Korean air space.

The woodlands gradually gave way to a series of small hills with streams running through their valleys, and further on, small villages on those streams. The land dipped down again, and me with it. Farmland appeared, small squares of marsh long converted into rice paddies. The land would be flat and straight out to the sea. I pushed the wheel forward and dropped down until the bottom of the fuselage was nearly touching the trees.

"Jesus," Andrea said, and closed her eyes.

"Relax. We're completely under control."

I switched the radio to the frequency used by the Russian pilots at Vladivostok. That channel was alive, too. We heard orders—frantic orders to scramble, and muttered compliances.

"They're after us!" Andrea said.

"You don't speak Russian. They're responding to the two Chinese squadrons chasing us. With any luck, they'll fly straight over us at something like forty thousand feet and not even give us a glance."

"Sure," she replied, with appropriate sarcasm.

I didn't believe it myself. But Vladivostok made no mention of a small, propeller-driven plane fleeing Manchuria just above the tree tops, and a half-second later, two dozen MIG-22's roared overhead, in formation and climbing at twenty thousand feet. If one of them noticed us, he failed to call home about it.

"It worked!" Andrea exclaimed. "They've gone to fight the Chinese!"

I patted her on the knee. "Keep your fingers crossed. It's time to call in the cavalry."

The medium peak of Sen-lin Shan slipped by to starboard. We were in Korean air space, just to their side of the border with Russia. I made a slight turn to port and turned the radio to the U.S. Navy frequency.

I radioed: "Hello Kennedy, hello Kennedy. this is Killmaster N3 calling with a mayday."

There was static, but no reply. I repeated the message, and finally the reply came:

"N3, this is the U.S.S. *John F. Kennedy*. What is your problem?"

"I am planning to ditch at sea approximately twenty-five miles southeast of Pos'yet. I am running low on fuel and will require a boat to pick up three persons and three large bags."

There was more waiting, then, "Ten-four, N3. A Sikorsky will drop a motor raft with a crew of two upon sighting your ditch. The destroyer Trenton will pick you up. Is there anything else?"

"Yeah, I wouldn't mind a little aerial display. That's just in case all these Oriental birds up in the air at the moment take notice of me."

"Air cover will be provided from fifteen miles out. Good luck, N3."

"Thanks," I said, and switched back to the channel for Vladivostok. As expected, they had been listening as well as talking. The air was suddenly alive with a good deal of curiosity about me.

They didn't have me on radar, which only seemed to make them madder. They knew from my transmission where I was going, but didn't know where I had come from. To his credit, the Russian commander in Vladivostok moved faster than his Chinese counterpart in Harbin. It took him three minutes to figure out I was fleeing Manchuria and another minute and a half to put it together with the widely-spreading news about the destruction of Trygda. Abruptly, the Russian C in C knew that the two Chinese squadrons were chasing my B.206 Beagle, not assaulting the frontier. He ordered his men to turn about and chase me instead.

"Damn," I said, and switched the radio back to the

American naval frequency operative in the Sea of Japan.

"Kennedy, this is N3 . . . the aerial display will definitely be needed."

"What's that mean?" Andrea asked as the acknowledgement came in from the aircraft carrier *Kennedy*.

"It means I'm asking our flyers to get their asses into the air and face off with theirs," I replied.

"And they're doing it?"

"They had better."

We passed over the railway line stretching from Pos'yet to Vladivostok. Dawn had broken, and peasants were stirring in the rice paddies and on the narrow, sandy roads of the coastal region.

Half a minute, and we were over the ocean. Andrea gasped in delight, and clapped her hands like a little girl. "We're safe!"

"We're safe at the twelve-mile limit, which is a bit over three minutes away at this speed."

"Come on, Nick . . . what can happen in three minutes?"

"Lots of things. Untie Rita."

"What?"

"We may have to swim. She can't do it with her hands and feet bound. And she's smart enough to realize that fighting us will do no good at this point. Aren't you, Rita?"

"I don't want to drown," Rita said.

"Untie her."

Andrea reluctantly did the job, and Rita rubbed the rope burns on her ankles and wrists.

"Thanks," she said.

"Don't mention it."

"When we ditch and wind up in the water, you wouldn't consider letting me swim back to Russia, would you?"

"Twenty-five miles?"

"They'll pick me up."

"In exchange for what?"

"In exchange for a favor in the future."

"I don't know."

"Come on, you'll need it. You have an ongoing relationship with us. Favors are needed on both sides. If not favors, then looking the other way."

"I'll think about it," I said.

"Think about this," Andrea said. "There is a lot of activity behind us."

I twisted around and through the port window could see a phalanx of Russian MIG-22 fighters closing on us.

The Russian squadron was five miles back and gaining with incredible speed. We were eight miles out, four miles from international waters (and air space), but the MIGs could catch us in something like fifteen seconds at Mach 1.5. Of course, so near to the line they would have to make at least a perfunctory challenge. I switched to the Russian frequency just in time to hear it.

"Unidentified aircraft, you will turn about and return to Russian soil."

I put on my best garrulous Moscow accent, and said in Russian, "What do you mean, turn about? Do you know who you're talking to, you fool?"

The silence lasted ten seconds, then a slightly uncertain voice came back. "Please identify."

"This is Marshall Sakharov! Do you mean you weren't informed I would be out here this morning teaching my son to fly? What is your name? I demand to know it!"

This time the silence lasted fully half a minute, by which time I was twelve miles out and out of Russian air space. Whether that nicety of international convention would be respected by them remained to be seen.

Marshall Sakharov was a petty functionary of the Russian version of our Joint Chiefs of Staff. He was a boozer and, as a general rule, not taken seriously. But he *did* fly, *did* have a son, and he *did* call east Siberia his homeland.

At least the captain in charge of the squadron of MIGs took

it seriously, until there came from Vladivostok the chilling message "Sakharov is in Moscow! Shoot him down!"

"He's in international territory," the hapless squadron leader shot back.

"Shoot him down!"

"Damn," I said and switching back to the frequency monitored by the *Kennedy*, broadcast, "That aerial display is way overdue."

"Coming, N3 . . . look up."

We were fifteen miles out. As promised, the aerial display materialized and it was beautiful—a dozen F-14's spread across the near horizon, welcoming us. They were flying low, toward us; the message was unmistakeable. I called the Vladivostok tower and said, "Killing me isn't worth what it would start."

For ten seconds, there was silence as the Russian and American squadrons roared head-on at one another. Then, without a word, the Russian planes turned back. Their captain had acted on his own. Within seconds, his decision was confirmed by the Vladivostok tower. "The plane is identified as a socialist patriot defecting from the reactionary Chinese air force," was the excuse.

Andrea hugged me and kissed me on the lips. "We did it."

"You have to be the luckiest man on the face of the earth," Rita said.

"If you think luck has anything to do with it, you're more an amateur than I thought," I replied.

The F-14's roared overhead, banked sharply, then headed back toward their carrier. Their leader called me and said, "We'll watch you, N3. Where do you want to ditch?"

"Wherever the water is soft. I'm flying on fumes. Where's the Sikorsky?"

"Overhead, N3. Just put the plane in the water and get ready."

We were twenty-five miles out to sea, and not far away was the sharp outline of an American destroyer with a bone in her teeth. My left engine sputtered, and then my right.

"Going down," I said, and my two passengers held on tight.

The Beagle slid down onto the surface of a mirror-calm sea, bounced twice, then came to a halt on top of three hundred fathoms of water in the Sea of Japan.

The B.206 Beagle had wings that were mounted at the base of the fuselage; they provided bouyancy in the water for perhaps two minutes. A plane with top-mounted wings would have deep-sixed within seconds.

I kicked open the door. Overhead, the large Navy helicopter swept down on us. In half a minute, an eight-man raft was in the water, a twenty-five horsepower outboard holding it alongside. I helped Andrea and Rita into it, and passed down the three bags and Pendle's body. I was the last in, and stepped into the raft just as the Beagle slipped beneath the surface of the sea, never to be seen again.

"What about it?" Rita asked. "I can swim. If I don't make it, at least I can die with dignity."

I smiled with shameful glee, and said, "Frankly, my dear, I don't give a damn what happens to you," and tied her up again.

The *Kennedy* rolled ever-so-slightly in the little swells which moved across the Sea of Japan. The room given me in the junior officers' quarters was small, but well lit and, most importantly, private. I wanted a few days to catch up on my sleep.

It was in the middle of the second day. I lay in the bunk staring at the ceiling, and wondering whether to go up on deck or stay in bed and go back to sleep. My question was soon answered: Hawk was there. I heard his footsteps and, the second the door to my compartment swung open, smelled the ever-present cigar.

I started to get to my feet, but he waved me to stay down. I sat on the edge of the bed.

"Well, I'll be damned. Nick Carter sleeping alone."

"This is a Navy ship, sir. They made her bunk down with a female midshipman."

"Sorry, Nick. I'll fix it for you if you like."

I shook my head. "I welcome the peace and quiet," I said. "Besides, Andrea is preoccupied with her rocks. She's got them arranged on the floor in a corner of the hangar deck, amusing the engineers and pilots."

"She really came through for you."

"Yeah. You ought to increase her funding."

"I'm trying to work out a deal where she can go back to the site. It will involve giving the bastards some of the lidanium. Not half, by any means, but some. The latest word from the geniuses in Washington is that the sons-of-bitches won't be able to put it to use anyway."

"The Chinese don't know she was in on it," I said. "Do you want the stuff?"

"What the hell do you think I came here fore? To see if you were okay?"

I smiled, and pulled the lidanium out from under my bunk. I had put it back in another lead-lined bag once we were aboard the carrier. I now removed it and placed the chunk of heavy metal in Hawk's outstretched hands. He hefted it, nodding as if suitably impressed.

"So this is it?"

"That's it?"

"Is it dangerous?"

"Not to me. At least not very much. A number of guys from the other side wouldn't agree, though."

He put it into its bag, and tucked that into a heavy black briefcase. "Your other friend . . . what was her name?"

"Rita."

"She's keeping her mouth shut, but we did finally manage to get a line on her. Her real name is Fala Dragomirov, from a Russian family transplanted to Finland around the time of the Bolshevik revolution. She went to school in Leningrad and was recruited by the KGB at the age of nineteen. She's been on two small assignments for them, one in the Baltic and the other in Marseilles. I don't know the details yet. You were her first big fish.''

"Thanks," I said, disliking the characterization.

"Don't mention it. Anyway, we hope to get useful information from her. That failing, she'll most likely be traded. They're holding a cipher clerk from our consulate in Leningrad . . . no doubt for just such an occasion.''

I yawned, stood up and stretched.

"If you're bored,'' Hawk said, "I can think of something for you to do.''

"Let me have a few more days of boredom.''

"Take a week. I have some business in Seoul and will be tied up for a while. Be in my office a week from tomorrow at 11:30. No . . . make it 12:30. We'll have lunch.''

"Sure.''

"I have to go. The chopper is waiting. What are your plans, N3?''

"I have to go to England. Pendle had a sister.''

Hawk smiled, and pulled from his jacket pocket a slip of paper. He gave it to me.

"Her name and address,'' he said. "She's been told of his death, but I don't think she'd mind hearing from you. When are you going?''

"Tomorrow, with the body. I'd like to take Andrea. She's never seen the English countryside.''

"On your own tab,'' Hawk smiled, then shook my hand and was gone.

I lay back down for a moment, and thought again of going back to sleep.

Abruptly, I got up, pulled on my clothes and went down to the hangar deck to check up on the march of science.

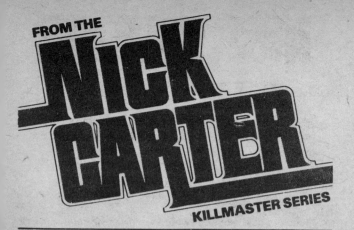

FROM THE NICK CARTER

KILLMASTER SERIES

☐ **TEMPLE OF FEAR**	80215-X	$1.75
☐ **THE NICHOVEV PLOT**	57435-1	$1.75
☐ **TIME CLOCK OF DEATH**	81025-X	$1.75
☐ **UNDER THE WALL**	84499-6	$1.75
☐ **THE PEMEX CHART**	65858-X	$1.95
☐ **SIGN OF THE PRAYER SHAWL**	76355-3	$1.75
☐ **THUNDERSTRUCK IN SYRIA**	80860-3	$1.95
☐ **THE MAN WHO SOLD DEATH**	51921-0	$1.75
☐ **THE SUICIDE SEAT**	79077-1	$2.25
☐ **SAFARI OF SPIES**	75330-2	$1.95
☐ **TURKISH BLOODBATH**	82726-8	$2.25
☐ **WAR FROM THE CLOUDS**	87192-5	$2.25
☐ **THE JUDAS SPY**	41295-5	$1.75

 ACE CHARTER BOOKS
P.O. Box 400, Kirkwood, N.Y. 13795   N-01

Please send me the titles checked above. I enclose _____.
Include 75¢ for postage and handling if one book is ordered; 50¢ per
book for two to five. If six or more are ordered, postage is free. California, Illinois, New York and Tennessee residents please add sales tax.

NAME_____

ADDRESS_____

CITY_____STATE_____ZIP_____

Page-turning Suspense from

CHARTER BOOKS

CHARTER BOOKS
Suspense to Keep You
On the Edge of Your Seat

CHARTER BOOKS
Excitement, Adventure
and Information
in these latest Bestsellers